W

or The Memory of Childhood

Les Choses. Une Histoire des années soixante
(Prix Renaudot 1965)
Quel petit vélo à guidon chromé au fond de las cour?
Un Homme qui dort
La Disparition
La Boutique obscure. 124 rêves
Espèces d'espaces
Alphabets
Je me souviens
La Vie mode d'emploi
(Prix Médicis 1978)
Translated as LIFE A USER'S MANUAL
Un Cabinet d'amateur
La Clôture et autres poèmes
Théâtre I
Tentative d'épuisement d'un lieu parisien
Penser/Classer

or

THE MEMORY OF CHILDHOOD

Georges Perec

Translated by David Bellos

DAVID R. GODINE · PUBLISHER
BOSTON

First published in English in 1988 by
David R. Godine, Publisher, Inc.
Horticultural Hall
300 Massachusetts Avenue
Boston, Massachusetts 02115

Originally published in 1975 by Editions Denoël

Copyright © 1975 by Editions Denoël
Translation copyright © 1988 by David R. Godine and
William Collins Sons & Co. Ltd

LIBRARY OF CONGRESS CATALOGING IN PUBLICATION DATA

Perec, Georges, 1936–1982
W, or the Memory of Childhood
Translation of: W, ou le souvenir d'enfance
I. Title. II. Title: W. III. Title: Childhood Memory
PQ2676.E67W213   1988   843'.914   88-45291
ISBN 0-87923-756-2

First edition
Photoset in Linotron Bembo by
Rowland Phototypesetting Ltd, Bury St Edmunds, Suffolk, England
Printed in the United States of America

The twenty-third letter of the alphabet is written in French, as in English, as a double V; and in French the letter "W" is also called "*double-vé*". The title of Perec's double tale of the Olympic ideal and of the discovery of a lost childhood thus has nothing to do with the sound of the letter U; it's not 'dʌbəl. juː (or dɒ.b'l‚yū) that is meant to echo through these pages, but 'dʌbəl. viː (or dɒ.b'l‚vē).

D.B.

In this book there are two texts which simply alternate; you might almost believe they had nothing in common, but they are in fact inextricably bound up with each other, as though neither could exist on its own, as though it was only their coming together, the distant light they cast on each other, that could make apparent what is never quite said in one, never quite said in the other, but said only in their fragile over-lapping.

One of these texts is entirely imaginary: it's an adventure story, an arbitrary but careful reconstruction of a childhood fantasy about a land in thrall to the Olympic ideal. The other text is an autobiography: a fragmentary tale of a wartime childhood, a tale lacking in exploits and memories, made up of scattered oddments, gaps, lapses, doubts, guesses and meagre anecdotes. Next to it, the adventure story is rather grandiose, or maybe dubious. For it begins to tell one tale, and then, all of a sudden, launches into another. In this break, in this split suspending the story on an unidentifiable expectation, can be found the point of departure for the whole of this book: the *points of suspension* on which the broken threads of childhood and the web of writing are caught.

G.P.

for E

PART ONE

That mindless mist where shadows swirl,
how could I pierce it?

RAYMOND QUENEAU

ONE

For years I put off telling the tale of my voyage to W. Today, impelled by a commanding necessity and convinced that the events to which I was witness must be revealed and brought to light, I resolve to defer it no longer. I do not conceal from myself the scruples – for some reason I was about to say: the pretexts – which seemed to argue against publication. For years I wished to keep the secret of what I had seen; it was not for me to divulge anything whatsoever about the mission which had been entrusted to me, first because the mission had, perhaps, not been accomplished – but who could have brought it off? – and then because he who entrusted it to me, he too has disappeared.

I wavered for years. Gradually, I forgot the uncertain adventures of the voyage. But those ghost towns, those bloody contests (I believed I could still hear the shouting), those unfurled, wind-whipped banners came back to live in my dreams. Incomprehension, horror and fascination commingled in the bottomless pit of those memories.

For years I sought out traces of my history, looking up maps and directories and piles of archives. I found nothing, and it sometimes seemed as though I had dreamt, that there had been only an unforgettable nightmare.

. . . years ago, in Venice, in a cheap restaurant in the Giudecca, I saw a man come in whom I thought I recognized. As I rushed

3

towards him, I was already fumbling my apologies. There could be no survivor. What my eyes had seen had really happened: the lianas had unseated the foundations, the forest had consumed the houses; sand overran the stadiums, cormorants swooped down in their thousands, and then silence, sudden icy silence. Whatever may happen now, whatever I may now do, I was the sole depository, the only living memory, the only vestige of that world. That, more than any other consideration, was what made me decide to write.

The attentive reader will have grasped no doubt from what has been said so far that in what I am about to relate I was a witness and not an actor. I am not the hero of my tale. Nor am I exactly its bard. Though the events I saw convulsed my previously insignificant existence, though their full weight still bears upon my conduct, upon my way of seeing, in recounting them I wish to adopt the cold, impassive tone of the ethnologist: I visited this sunken world and this is what I saw there. I am not possessed with the boiling fury of Ahab, but with Ishmael's white reverie, with the patience of Bartleby. Once again, as for so many before me, these latter shall be my guiding spirits.

However, so as not to infringe an almost universal rule and one which in any case I have no wish to dispute, I shall now indicate as concisely as I can certain features of my existence and, more particularly, the circumstances which prompted my voyage.

I was born on 25 June 19.. around four o'clock, at R., a hamlet of three houses, not far from A. My father owned a small farm. He died from complications arising from an injury when I was nearly six years old. He left almost nothing but debts, and my whole inheritance came to a few possessions, some linen, three or four pieces of crockery. One of my father's two neighbours

*volunteered to adopt me; I grew up amongst his people, half a
son, half a farmhand.*

*At the age of sixteen I left R. and went to the town; I plied
various trades for a time, but as I found none I liked, I ended up
enlisting. Accustomed as I was to obedience, and possessing an
unusually sturdy constitution, I could have made a good soldier,
but I soon realized that I would never really adapt to military
life. After a year spent in France at the Training Centre at T.,
I was sent on active service; I stayed more than fifteen months.
At V., whilst on leave, I deserted. With the assistance of an
organization of conscientious objectors, I succeeded in reaching
Germany where for many years I was without work. In the end
I settled at H., right next to the border with Luxemburg. I found
a job as a mechanic in the largest garage in the town. I lodged in
a small family hotel and spent most of my evenings in a bar
watching television or, occasionally, playing backgammon with
one or another of my workmates.*

TWO

I have no childhood memories. Up to my twelfth year or thereabouts, my story comes to barely a couple of lines: I lost my father at four, my mother at six; I spent the war in various boarding houses at Villard-de-Lans. In 1945, my father's sister and her husband adopted me.

For years, I took comfort in such an absence of history: its objective crispness, its apparent obviousness, its innocence protected me; but what did they protect me from, if not precisely from my history, the story of my living, my real story, my own story, which presumably was neither crisp nor objective, nor apparently obvious, nor obviously innocent?

"I have no childhood memories": I made this assertion with confidence, with almost a kind of defiance. It was nobody's business to press me on this question. It was not a set topic on my syllabus. I was excused: a different history, History with a capital H, had answered the question in my stead: the war, the camps.

When I was thirteen I made up a story which I told and drew in pictures. Later I forgot it. Seven years ago, one evening, in Venice, I suddenly remembered that this story was called W and that it was, in a way, if not the story of my childhood, then at least a story of my childhood.

Apart from the title thus wrested back, I had practically no memory of W. All I knew of it came to a couple of lines:

it was about the life of a community concerned exclusively with sport, on a tiny island off Tierra del Fuego.

Once again the snares of writing were set. Once again I was like a child playing hide-and-seek, who doesn't know what he fears or wants more: to stay hidden, or to be found.

Later I came across some of the drawings I had done around the age of thirteen. With their help I reinvented W and wrote it, publishing it as I wrote, in serial form, in *La Quinzaine littéraire* between September 1969 and August 1970.

Today, four years later, I propose to bring to term – by which I mean just as much "to mark the end of" as "to give a name too" – this gradual unravelling. W is no more like my Olympic fantasy than that Olympic fantasy was like my childhood. But in the crisscross web they weave as in my reading of them I know there is to be found the inscription and the description of the path I have taken, the passage of my history and the story of my passage.

THREE

I had been at H. for three years when, on the morning of 26 July 19.., my landlady handed me a letter. It had been posted the previous day from K., a fairly large town about 50 kilometres from H. I opened the letter; it was written in French. The paper, of very high quality, had a letterhead bearing the name

OTTO APFELSTAHL, MD

above a complicated coat of arms, excellently engraved, but which my ignorance of heraldry did not allow me to identify, or even, quite simply, to decipher. In fact I succeeded in recognizing clearly only two of the five symbols which composed it: a crenellated tower, in the middle, going the full height of the crest and, at the bottom on the right, an open book, with blank pages; the other three, despite the efforts I made to understand them, remained obscure to me. Yet it was not a matter of abstract symbols; they were not chevrons, for example, or stripes or lozenges, but figures that were somehow double, with precise but ambiguous designs which seemed to be open to several different interpretations, without it being possible to decide on a satisfactory choice: one of them could just about have been a sinuous serpent with bay leaves for scales, another might have been a hand that was simultaneously a root; the third was equally a nest and a brazier, or a crown of thorns, or a burning bush, or even an impaled heart.

There was no address and no telephone number. The letter said only this:

Sir,
We should be most grateful if you would kindly agree to meet us to discuss a matter which concerns you.
We shall be at the Berghof Hotel, 18 Nürnbergstrasse, this Friday 27 July and shall await you in the bar from 6 p.m.
Thanking you in advance, and with our apologies for not being able to give you a fuller explanation at the present time, we remain,
Yours faithfully . . .

There followed a more or less illegible signature which only the name given in the letterhead allowed me to identify as "O. Apfelstahl"
It is easy to understand that this letter scared me at first. My first thought was to run away: I had been recognized; it had to be blackmail. Later I contrived to master my fear: that the letter was written in French did not mean that it was intended for me, for the man I had been, for the deserter; my current identity established me as a French-speaking Swiss, so my command of the language was not likely to surprise anyone. The people who had given me assistance did not know my former name, and thus it would require an improbable, inexplicable set of coincidences for anyone who had met me in my previous life to find me and recognize me now. H. is only a small town, off the main roads, unknown to tourists, and I spent the best part of my days down in the inspection pit or on my back underneath an engine. And even if, by some unbelievable chance, someone had come across my tracks, what could he ask from me? I had no money, I had no way of getting any. The war in which I had fought had been

9

over for five years; it was more than likely that I had even been amnestied.

I tried to imagine, with as much calm as I could muster, all the possible ramifications of the letter. Was it the outcome of a lengthy, painstaking investigation, of an enquiry which had gradually drawn its net around me? Was it written to a man whose name I might have or who had my name? Was it from a solicitor who believed he had found in me the heir to a huge fortune?

I read the letter again and again, and tried each time to find another clue, but all I found were grounds for still greater perplexity. Was the letter's "we" merely a formality, the customary style of almost all business correspondence, where the signatory speaks for and on behalf of his employers, or was I dealing with two, or more, correspondents? And what was the meaning of the "MD" which followed the name of Otto Apfelstahl in the letterhead? In theory, according to the reference book I borrowed briefly from the garage secretary, it could only be the American abbreviation for "Medical Doctor", but though the symbol was widely used in the United States, there was no reason for it to appear in the letterhead of a German, even if he were a doctor; otherwise I should have to suppose that this Otto Apfelstahl, though he wrote to me from K., was not German but an American. That would not in itself have been particularly surprising – there are many German émigrés in America, and many American doctors are of German or Austrian descent; but what could an American doctor want of me, and why had he come to K.? Was it even imaginable that a doctor of any nationality would use a letterhead which indicated his profession, but instead of supplying the information one would have a right to expect – his own or his surgery's address and telephone number, his consulting times, his hospital posts, etc. – furnished only a fusty and impenetrable crest?

All day I pondered on what I ought to do. Should I keep the appointment? Or should I run away right then and start all over again, somewhere else, in Australia or in Argentina, living another illegal existence, with another fragile alibi, with another fabricated past and another identity? As time passed my anxiety gave way to impatience and curiosity; feverishly I imagined that this meeting would change my life.

I spent some of the evening at the Municipal Library, leafing through dictionaries, encyclopaedias, and directories, in the hope of gleaning information about Otto Apfelstahl or possible clues to other acceptations of the initials "MD" or to the meaning of the crest. But I found nothing.

The next morning, a lingering presentiment made me stuff into my travelling bag some linen and what I might have called, were they not quite so paltry, my most treasured possessions: my wireless, a silver fob watch which might well have been my great-grandfather's, a little mother-of-pearl figurine bought in V., a rare and peculiar seashell which my "godmother" correspondent had sent me when I was on active service. Did I mean to run away? I don't think so; rather, to be ready for any eventuality. I gave my landlady notice that I would be away for perhaps a few days and settled up with her. I went to see my employer. I told him that my mother had died and I had to go and arrange the funeral at D., in Bavaria. He allowed me a week off and, as it was nearly the end of the month, gave me my pay a few days early.

I went to the station and put my bag in an automatic locker. Then I sat in the second-class waiting room, almost in the middle of a group of Portuguese workers leaving for Hamburg, and I waited for six o'clock in the evening.

FOUR

I don't know where the break is in the threads that tie me
to my childhood. Like everyone else, or almost everyone,
I had a father and a mother, a potty, a cot, a rattle, and,
later on, a bicycle which apparently I never mounted
without screaming with terror at the mere thought that
someone might try to raise or even remove the two small
side-wheels which kept me stable. Like everyone else, I
have forgotten everything about the earliest years of my
existence.

My childhood belongs to those things which I know I
don't know much about. It is behind me; yet it is the
ground on which I grew, and it once belonged to me,
however obstinately I assert that it no longer does. For
years I tried to sidetrack or to cover up these obvious facts,
and I wrapped myself in the harmless status of the orphan,
the unparented, the nobody's boy. However, childhood is
neither longing nor terror, neither a paradise lost nor
the Golden Fleece, but maybe it is a horizon, a point of
departure, a set of co-ordinates from which the axes of my
life may draw their meaning. Even if I have the help only
of yellowing snapshots, a handful of eyewitness accounts
and a few paltry documents to prop up my implausible
memories, I have no alternative but to conjure up what for
too many years I called the irrevocable: the things that
were, the things that stopped, the things that were closed

off – things that surely were and today are no longer, but things that also were so that I may still be.

★

My two earliest memories are not entirely implausible, even though, obviously, the many variations and imaginary details I have added in the telling of them – in speech or in writing – have altered them greatly, if not completely distorted them.

The earlier memory is apparently set in the back room of my grandmother's shop. I am three. I am sitting in the middle of the room with Yiddish newspapers scattered around me. The family circle surrounds me wholly, but the sensation of encirclement does not cause me any fear or feeling of being smothered; on the contrary, it is warm, protective, loving: all the family – the entirety, the totality of the family – is there, gathered like an impregnable battlement around the child who has just been born (but didn't I say a moment ago that I was three?).

Everyone is in raptures over the fact that I have pointed to a Hebrew character and called it by its name: the sign was supposedly shaped like a square with a gap in its lower left-hand corner, something like ‏ק‏ and its name was apparently gammeth, or gammel.[1] The subject, the softness, the lighting of the whole scene are, for me, reminiscent of a painting, maybe a Rembrandt or maybe an invented one, which might have been called "Jesus amid the Doctors".[2]

The second memory is briefer; it is more like a dream. It strikes me as even more obviously elaborated than the first; several versions of it exist, and overlaid upon one another,

13

they make the memory itself more illusory. The simplest statement of it would be this: my father comes home from his work; he gives me a key. In one version, the key is made of gold. In another version it is not a golden key, but a gold coin; in yet another version, I am on the potty when my father comes home from his work; and, finally, in yet another version, I swallow the coin, everyone fusses, and the next day it turns up in my stool.

1. Excess detail such as this is all that is needed to ruin the memory or in any case to burden it with a letter it did not possess. There is in fact a letter called "Gimmel" which I like to think could be the initial of my first name; it looks absolutely nothing like the sign I have drawn which could just about masquerade as a "mem" or "M". My aunt Esther told me recently that in 1939 – I was three then – my aunt Fanny, my mother's younger sister, used to take me from Belleville to see her. At that time Esther was living in Rue des Eaux, very near Avenue de Versailles. We used to go to play on the banks of the Seine, next to the great piles of sand; one of my games consisted of making out, with Fanny, the letters not in Yiddish but in French newspapers.

2. In this memory or pseudo-memory, Jesus is a newborn infant surrounded by kindly old men. All the paintings entitled "Jesus amid the Doctors" depict him as an adult. The picture I am referring to here, if it exists, is much more likely to be a "Presentation in the Temple".

FIVE

It was precisely six o'clock when I went through the revolving door into the Berghof Hotel. The lobby was more or less deserted; casually leaning against a column, with their arms crossed, three bellboys dressed in red, gilt-buttoned waistcoats were chatting in low voices. The porter, recognizable by his huge bottle-green greatcoat and his plumed coachman's hat, was crossing the lobby diagonally, carrying two hefty suitcases and leading the way for a female guest who held a small dog in her arms.

The bar was at the end of the lobby, barely separated from it by a lattice-work partition decorated with tall green plants. To my great surprise, there were no customers in the bar; no cigar smoke hung in the air to make the atmosphere almost opaque and somewhat stifling; instead of the muffled confusion I had expected, the noise of a score of conversations over insipid background music, there were only cleared tables neatly set out with place mats and gleaming brass ashtrays. The air conditioning made the place almost chilly. Sitting behind a counter of dark wood and steel, a barman in a slightly crumpled jacket was reading the Frankfurter Zeitung.

I went to sit at the back of the room. The barman raised his eyes momentarily from his newspaper and threw me a questioning glance; I ordered a beer. He brought it to me, dragging his feet; I noticed he was a very old man; his really very wrinkled hand shook a little.

"Not many people about," I said, half just to say something and half because it really did perplex me.

15

He nodded then suddenly asked me: "Do you want some pretzels?"

"Excuse me?" I said, not grasping.

"Pretzels. Pretzels to eat with your beer."

"No thank you. I never eat pretzels. Give me a newspaper instead."

He turned about, but evidently I had expressed myself badly, or he had not paid attention because, instead of going over to the newspaper racks hanging on the wall, he went back to his counter, put down his tray, and went out through a little door which must have given access to the pantry.

I looked at my watch. Only five past six. I got up and went to fetch a newspaper. It was the weekly financial supplement to a Luxemburg daily, the Luxemburger Wort, more than two months out of date. I glanced through it for a good ten minutes as I drank my beer, quite alone in the bar.

You could not say that Otto Apfelstahl was late; neither could you say that he was on time. All you could say, all you could surmise, all I could surmise, was that with any appointment you had to allow a quarter of an hour for waiting around. I should not have needed to reassure myself, I had no reason to be anxious, but nonetheless Otto Apfelstahl's absence made me uneasy. It was after six o'clock and I was in the bar waiting for him, whereas he should have been in the bar himself, waiting for me.

Towards twenty past six – I had abandoned the paper and finished my beer long since – I decided to leave. Perhaps there was a message for me from Otto Apfelstahl at the reception desk, perhaps he was expecting me in one of the reading rooms, or in the lobby, or in his room; perhaps he was calling it off and proposing to defer the discussion until later? Suddenly there was a kind of hubbub in the lobby: five or six people burst noisily into the bar and sat down at a table. Almost simultaneously two bartenders emerged from behind the counter. They were young and I could not help noticing that the two put together would just about have made up the age of the man who had served me.

It was just as I was calling one of the waiters so I could pay for my drink – though he seemed too busy taking the orders of the new customers to pay any attention to me – that Otto Apfelstahl appeared: a man who stops almost as soon as he has entered a public place, looks all around with particular care, with an air of attentive inquisitiveness, and strides forward as soon as his eye meets yours, such a man can only be your opposite number.

He was a man of around forty, quite short, very thin, with a narrow, sharp-featured face and greying, crew-cut hair. He wore a dark-grey twill suit. In so far as you can tell a man's profession by his appearance, he struck me as being not a doctor but rather a businessman, a senior bank manager or a lawyer.

He stopped a few inches from me.

"You are Gaspard Winckler?" he asked me, but actually the sentence was barely a question, it was more a statement of fact.

"Er . . . Yes . . .," I replied idiotically, and made to stand up, but he stopped me with a wave of his hand.

"No, do stay seated: we shall be much more comfortable talking if we sit."

He sat down. He considered my empty glass for a second.

"You like beer, I see."

"Sometimes," I said, not really knowing what to answer.

"I prefer tea."

He turned slightly towards the counter, half raising a finger. The waiter descended straightaway.

"A pot of tea for me. Would you like another beer?" he asked of me.

I acquiesced.

"And a beer for the gentleman."

I was increasingly uneasy. Should I ask him if he was called

17

Otto Apfelstahl? Should I ask him point blank what he wanted of me? I got out my packet of cigarettes and offered him one, but he refused.

"I smoke only cigars, and only after my evening meal."

"Are you a doctor?"

Contrary to my naïve expectation, he seemed not at all surprised by my question. He gave but the merest smile.

"In what way does the fact that I smoke a cigar only after my evening meal lead you to think that I might be a doctor?"

"Because that is one of the questions I have had in my mind since I received your letter."

"Do you have many others in mind?"

"Yes, some."

"And what are they?"

"Well, for instance, what do you want of me?"

"That is indeed an obvious question. Do you wish me to answer it straightaway?"

"I should be most grateful."

"May I first ask you another question?"

"Go ahead."

"Did you ever wonder what became of the person who gave you your name?"

"I beg your pardon?" I said, not grasping.

SIX

I was born on Saturday, 7 March 1936, towards nine in the evening, in a maternity clinic located at 19 Rue de l'Atlas, in the xixth *arrondissement* of Paris. My father, I believe, was the one who went to register me at the *mairie*. He gave me only one forename – Georges – and declared me to be French.[1] Both he and my mother were Polish. My father was not quite twenty-seven and my mother was not yet twenty-three. They had been married for a year and a half. Apart from the fact that they lived a few yards from each other, I don't know quite what circumstances led to their meeting. I was their first child. They had a second, in 1938 or 1939, a little girl whom they named Irène, but she lived for only a few days.[2]

For years I thought that Hitler had marched into Poland on 7 March 1936. I was wrong, about the date or about the country, but that's of no real importance. Hitler was already in power and the camps were working very smoothly. It wasn't Warsaw Hitler was taking, but it could have been, or it could have been the Danzig Corridor, or Austria, or the Saar, or Czechoslovakia. What is certain is that a story had already begun, a history which for me and for all my people was soon to become a matter of life and for the most part a matter of death.[3]

1. In fact the declaration made in accordance with clause 3 of the Law of 10 August 1927 was entered by my father a few months later, on 17 August 1936 to be precise, in the presence of the justice of the peace of the xxth *arrondissement*. I possess an authenticated copy of this declaration, typed in violet on a letter-card dated 23 September 1942 and posted the following day by my mother to her sister-in-law Esther, which constitutes the last proof I have of my mother's existence.

2. According to my aunt Esther, as far as I know the only person who can now remember the existence of her only niece (her brother Léon had three boys), Irène was born in 1937 and died a few weeks later from a malformation of the stomach.

3. To clear my conscience I looked in newspapers of the period (mainly the issues of *Le Temps* for 7 and 8 March 1936) to find out exactly what was happening on that day:

Berlin Spectacular! Locarno Pact denounced by Third Reich! German troops enter the Rhineland DMZ.
In an American daily, Stalin denounces Germany as a warmonger.
Caretakers strike in New York.
Italian–Abyssinian campaign. Possible start of negotiations for an end to hostilities.
Crisis in Japan.
Electoral reform in France.
Germany negotiates with Lithuania.
Trial in Bulgaria following disaffection in the army.
Carlos Prestes arrested in Brazil; allegedly denounced by an American communist who subsequently took his own life.

Communist troops advance in northern China.

Italians bomb military hospitals in Abyssinia.

Kosher slaughtering banned in Poland.

Nazis convicted and sentenced for plotting outrages in Austria.

Attempt on life of Yugoslav premier: parliamentarian Arnaoutovic fires at but misses Premier Stojadinovic.

Incidents at the Paris Law Faculty. M. Jèze's lecture interrupted by stink bombs.

Counter-demonstration by the Federal Union of Students and Neutralist Students.

Renault produces the Nerva sports model.

Full-length production of *Tristan and Isolde* at the Paris Opera.

Florent Schmitt elected to the French Institute.

Commemoration of the centenary of the death of Ampère.

In the semi-final of the French Football Cup, Charleville meets Red Star and the winners of Sochaux vs Fives meet the winners of the Racing vs Lille.

Plan for a Broadcasting House.

Gibbs recommends Gibbs shaving cream for oily skin: and for dry skins, Gibbs soap-free rapidshave.

Scarface showing at the Ursulines.

Chapayev on at the Panthéon cinema.

Samson on at the Paramount.

La Guerre de Troie n'aura pas lieu at the Athénée theatre, and at the Madeleine, *Anne-Marie*, by Raymond Bernard, from an idea by Antoine de Saint-Exupéry, with Annabella and Pierre-Richard Wilm. Advertised to open on Friday 13 March: *Modern Times*, by Charlie Chaplin.

SEVEN

"You do not understand?" Otto Apfelstahl *asked after a moment's pause, as he looked at me over his teacup.*

"Let us say your question is ambiguous, to say the least."

"Ambiguous?"

"There is more than one person who, as you put it, gave me my name."

"Since you think it necessary, I shall make my question more precise. I am not alluding to your father, nor to any member of your family or your community after whom you might have been named, as is, I believe, still a fairly widespread custom. Nor am I thinking of any of the people who, five years ago, helped you to acquire your current identity. I mean, quite straightforwardly, the person whose name you have."

"The person whose name I have!"

"You did not know him?"

"Indeed I did not. And what is he doing?"

"We would very much like to know. That is in fact the sole purpose of this meeting."

"I do not see any way in which I could be of use to you. I always thought that the papers I had been given were forged."

"At the time, Gaspard Winckler was a child of eight. He was deaf and dumb. His mother, Caecilia, was a world-famous Austrian singer who had escaped to Switzerland during the war. Gaspard was a sickly, puny boy, condemned by his disability to virtually total isolation. He spent most of his time crouching in a corner of his bedroom, ignoring the sumptuous toys and presents

that his mother or family acquaintances gave him day in day out, and almost always refusing to eat. His mother, in despair, decided to try to overcome her son's helplessness by taking him around the world; she thought that new horizons, changes of climate and tempo would have a beneficial effect on her son and might even set in train a process leading to the recovery of hearing and speech, since all the doctors they had consulted were quite clear on this point: there was no internal injury, no inherited disorder, no anatomical or physiological deformity to account for the boy being deaf and dumb; this could only be ascribed to some infantile trauma whose precise configuration unfortunately remained obscure despite examinations by numerous psychiatrists. All this, you may well say, does not have much to do with your own adventure and still does not tell you how you came to have the same identity as this poor child. To understand that, you should appreciate first that out of both caution and preference for neat work, the support organization which took care of you did not use forged papers, but only genuine passports, identity cards and stamps, all supplied by officials in sympathy with its cause. It so happens that the Genevan official who was going to deal with your case died three days before you got to Switzerland, before he had anything ready, but after all the stop-overs and stages of your subsequent journey had been set up. The organization was at a loss. That is when Caecilia Winckler came into the picture; she belonged to the organization, and was in fact one of its main officials in Switzerland. And that is why, since it was an emergency, you were given the scarcely amended passport which Caecilia had had issued a few weeks earlier for her own son."

"And what about him?"

"International agreements allow for a child who is still a minor to be included in the passport of one parent."

"But what would have happened later?"

"Nothing, I imagine. They would have done whatever was

23

necessary for Gaspard to obtain another passport; I do not think they ever dreamt of asking to have yours back one day."

"So why do you think that I might have met them?"

"Did I ever say anything of the sort? You have to let me finish. A few weeks after you had been through Geneva, when we were certain you were out of danger, Caecilia and Gaspard left for Trieste, where they embarked on an eighty-five-foot yacht, the Sylvander, *a superb vessel which could take them through the worst typhoons. There were six of them on board: Caecilia, Gaspard, Hugh Barton (a friend of Caecilia's and who was in a sense the commanding officer), two Maltese sailors who also served as ship's steward and cook, and a young tutor, Angus Pilgrim, a specialist in the education of the deaf and dumb. Contrary to Caecilia's hopes, the voyage does not seem to have improved Gaspard's condition: most of the time he stayed in his cabin and only very rarely agreed to come up on deck to look at the sea. From the letters which Caecilia, Hugh Barton, Angus Pilgrim and even Zeppo and Felipe, the two sailors, wrote during that time, and which I came to consult for reasons you will shortly understand, there emerges over the months a great sense of poignancy: the voyage, intended to be a cure, progressively loses its* raison d'être; *it becomes increasingly obvious that it has been a useless undertaking, but neither is there any point in bringing it to an end; the boat wanders before the wind, from one shore to another, from port to port, stopping a month here, three months there, searching ever more vainly for the place, the creek, the vista, the beach, the pier where the miracle could happen; and the strangest part is that the longer the voyage goes on, the more convinced everyone aboard seems to become that such a place exists, that there is, somewhere on the ocean, an isle or atoll, a rock or headland where suddenly it could all happen – the veil sundered, the light turned on; that all that is needed is a rather special sunrise, or sunset, or any sublime or even trivial event, a*

flight of birds, a school of whales, rain, a doldrum, the torpor of a torrid day. And each of them clings to this illusion, until one day, off Tierra del Fuego, they are hit by one of those sudden cyclones which are everyday occurrences in those parts, and the boat sinks."

EIGHT

I possess one photograph of my father and five of my
mother (on the back of the photograph of my father, one
evening when I was drunk, probably in 1955 or 1956, I
tried to chalk: "There is something rotten in the state of
Denmark." But I didn't even manage to scrawl to the end
of the fourth word). I have no memory of my father other
than the one about the key or coin he might have given me
one evening on his return from work. The only surviving
memory of my mother is of the day she took me to the
Gare de Lyon, which is where I left for Villard-de-Lans in
a Red Cross convoy: though I have no broken bones, I
wear my arm in a sling. My mother buys me a comic
entitled *Charlie and the Parachute*: on the illustrated cover,
the parachute's rigging lines are nothing other than
Charlie's trousers' braces.

★

The idea of writing the story of my past arose almost at
the same time as the idea of writing. The following two
passages date from more than fifteen years ago. I have
copied them out without making any changes; I have used
notes for the corrections and comments which I now feel
obliged to add.

1

The father in the photograph poses like a father. He is tall. He is bareheaded, holding his kepi in his hand. His greatcoat comes down very low.[1] It is gathered at the waist by one of those thick leather belts that remind you of the window straps in third-class railway carriages. Between the polished military boots – it is Sunday – and the hem of the greatcoat you can just make out that there are interminable puttees.

The father is smiling. He is a private. He is on leave in Paris; it is the end of winter, in the Bois de Vincennes.[2]

My father was a soldier for a very short time. Nonetheless, when I think of him, I always think of a soldier. He was a hairdresser, vaguely, and a caster and moulder, but I can never manage, so to speak, to see him as a working man.[3] One day I saw a picture of him in mufti and it quite astonished me; I had only ever known him as a soldier. For years I kept his photograph by my bed, in a leather frame which was one of the first presents I received after the war.[4]

I have much more information about my father than about my mother because I was adopted by my father's sister. I know where he was born, I could just about describe him, and I know how he was brought up; I know some of the traits of his character.

My father's sister was rich.[5] She was the first to come to France and brought over her parents and her two brothers. One of the latter went to seek his fortune in Israel.[6] That one was not my father. The other made a not too serious effort to establish himself in the diamond trade, to which his brother-in-law had introduced him, but after a few months of stone-setting he decided to give up the prospect of making his way in the world and became a skilled worker.[7]

What I like very much in my father is his jauntiness. I see a man whistling a tune. He had a nice name: André. But I was bitterly disappointed when I found out that in reality – that is, on official papers – his name was Icek Judko, which didn't mean very much.[8]

My aunt, who loved him dearly, who brought him up almost single-handed, and who solemnly vowed to take care of me (which she certainly did), told me once that he was a poet; that he played truant; that he didn't like to wear a tie; that he was more at ease with his pals than with diamond traders (which still doesn't tell me why he didn't pick his pals from the diamond trade).[9]

My father was also a doughty fighter. The day war broke out, he went to the recruiting office and enlisted. He was put in the Twelfth Foreign Regiment.

The memories I have of my father are not many.

At a particular time in my life, in fact at the time I referred to previously, the love I felt for my father became bound up with a passionate craze for tin soldiers. One day my aunt confronted me with a choice for Christmas between roller skates and a set of infantrymen. I chose the infantry; she didn't even bother to talk me out of it, went into the shop, and bought the skates, for which I took a long time to forgive her. Later, when I began going to grammar school, she used to give me two francs every morning (I think it was two francs) for the bus. But I pocketed the money and walked to school, which made me late, but enabled me three times a week to buy a toy soldier (made of clay, alas!) in a little shop on my way. Indeed, one day I saw in the window a crouching soldier carrying a field telephone. I remembered my father had been in the communications corps,[10] and this toy soldier, which I bought the very next day, became the regular centrepiece of all the tactical and strategic manoeuvres which I performed with my little army.

I thought up various glorious deaths for my father. The finest had him being cut down by a burst of machine-gun fire as he was bringing to General Soandso the dispatch containing news of victory.

I was rather silly. My father had died a slow and stupid death. It was on the day after the armistice.[11] He had got in the way of a stray shell. The hospital was overflowing. It has now reverted to being a deserted church in a lifeless little town. The cemetery is well maintained. In one corner of it there are a few rotting wooden stakes with names and numbers.

I once went to what you could call my father's grave. It was on a first of November. There was mud everywhere.[12]

Sometimes it seems to me that my father was not a fool. Then I tell myself that this kind of definition, positive or negative, doesn't get you very far. Nonetheless, I am comforted a little by knowing he possessed sensitivity and intelligence.

I don't know what my father would have done had he lived. The oddest thing is that his death, and my mother's, too often seems to me to be obvious. It's become part of the way things are.

Cyrla Schulevitz,[13] my mother, who, I learnt on the few occasions I heard her spoken of, was more usually called Cécile,[14] was born in Warsaw on 20 August 1913. Her father Aaron was a craftsman; her mother, Laja, née Klajnerer,[15] kept house. Cyrla was the third daughter of seven children.[16] Her birth exhausted her mother, and she had only one more daughter, born a year after my mother, and named Soura.[17]

These more or less statistical details, which are of fairly limited interest to me, are all that I have concerning the childhood and youth of my mother. Or rather, to be more precise, all that I can rely on. The rest, although it sometimes seems that someone told it to me, and that it comes from a trustworthy source, is probably ascribable to the quite extraordinary imaginary relationship which I regularly maintained with my maternal branch at a particular time in my brief existence.[18]

With that reservation, I shall therefore say that I suppose my mother's childhood to have been squalid and straightforward. Born in 1913, she could not avoid growing up in the war. And she was Jewish, and poor. She must have been clothed in the hand-me-downs of six siblings; she must have been left pretty much to herself, so the others could get on with laying the table, peeling the vegetables, washing up. When I think of her, I imagine a twisting ghetto street in a pale, sickly light, maybe snow, and dingy, poverty-stricken shops with endless, stationary queues. And my mother is in the midst of all that, knee-high to a grasshopper, a wee chit of a thing, wrapped four times round in a knitted shawl, hauling a great black shopping bag twice her own weight.[19]

Even so, I have spared her from thrashings, though I suspect that in the environment and the circumstances I have just sketched they must have been two a penny. On the contrary, I see great tenderness and great patience, a lot of love. My grandfather Aaron, whom I never knew, often takes on the mantle of a wise man. In the evening, after carefully tidying away his tools,[20] he dons steel-rimmed spectacles and chants the Bible out loud. The children are virtuous and placed around the table in order of height, and Laja takes the plates they hold out in turn, and pours into each a ladleful of soup.[21]

I don't see my mother growing older. The years pass by all the same; I don't know how she grew up; I know neither what she learnt nor what she thought. It seems to me as if for years things stayed what they always had been for her: poverty, fear, ignorance. Did she learn to read? I've no idea.[22] Sometimes I wish I knew, but there is too much now to distance me from these memories. The arbitrary, schematic image that I have of her suits me; her image fits and defines her for me almost perfectly.

There was just one event in my mother's life: one day she learnt she was to leave for Paris. I imagine her ecstatic. Somewhere she got hold of an atlas, a map, a picture; she saw the Eiffel Tower or the Arc de Triomphe. Perhaps she thought of heaps of things, probably not of fine dresses and balls, but maybe of the mild climate, the quiet, contentment. People must have told her there would be no more massacres and no more ghettos, and money for everyone.

So they left. I don't know when or how or why. Was it a pogrom that drove them out, or did someone bring them over?[23] I know that they got to Paris: her parents, herself, her younger sister Soura, maybe the others as well. They settled in the xxth *arrondissement*, in a street whose name I have forgotten.

Laja, the mother, died. I believe my mother learnt to be a hairdresser. Then she met my father. They married. She was twenty-one years and ten days old. It happened on 30 August 1934, at the registry office of the xxth. They moved into Rue Vilin; they managed a small hairdressing business.

I was born in the month of March 1936. Perhaps there were three years of relative happiness, no doubt darkened by baby's illnesses (whooping cough, measles, chickenpox),[24] various kinds of financial problems, a future that boded ill.

War came. My father enlisted and died. My mother became a war widow. She went into mourning. I was put out to a nanny. Her business was closed. She signed on as a worker in a factory making alarm clocks.[25] I seem to remember she injured herself one day and her hand was pierced through. She wore the star.

One day she took me to the station. It was in 1942. It was the Gare de Lyon. She bought me a magazine which must have been an issue of *Charlie*. As the train moved out, I caught sight of her, I seem to remember, waving a white handkerchief from the platform. I was going to Villard-de-Lans, with the Red Cross.

I've been told that later on she tried to cross the Loire. The runner she called on, who was to smuggle her across, and whose address had been passed on by her sister-in-law who was already in the free zone, turned out to be away. She didn't make a fuss and returned to Paris. She was advised to move house, to hide. She didn't bother. She thought her war widow's status would keep her out of trouble.[26] She was picked up in a raid, together with her sister, my aunt. She was interned at Drancy on 23 January 1943, then deported on 11 February following, destination Auschwitz. She saw the country of her birth again before she died. She died without understanding.

1. No, in fact, my father's greatcoat does not come very low: it goes down to the knee; and the tails, moreover, are gathered halfway up the thighs. It is therefore wrong to say you can "just make out" the existence of puttees: they are fully visible, as is the greater part of the trousers.

2. Sunday, leave, Bois de Vincennes: there's no basis for any of this. The third of the photographs I have of my mother – one of the ones where I am with her – was taken in the Bois de Vincennes. But nowadays I should rather say that this one was taken at the place where my father was actually stationed; to judge by its format (15.5 x 11.5 cm), it is not an amateur's snapshot: my father, in his virtually brand-new uniform, must have posed for one of those itinerant photographers who do the rounds of recruiting boards, barracks, weddings and schools at the end of the year.

3. My father came to France in 1926, a few months before his parents David and Rose (Rozja). Previously he had been apprenticed to a Warsaw hatter. His elder sister Esther (who subsequently adopted me) had been in Paris for five years already; he went to live with her for a time in Rue Lamartine, and apparently he learned French with great ease. Esther's husband David worked for a trader in real pearls, and it's not impossible that he suggested my father should work in the jewellery business. What is certain in any case is that Rose, a woman of great energy, opened a small grocery shop, and that my father worked for her: it was he who went to Les Halles in the small hours to fetch the produce. It's probably true that he was also, and maybe simultaneously, a worker: several documents have him down as a "metal turner", but I don't know whether he was in a factory or in a small business of his own. He may have worked in a baker's in Rue Cadet as well, in a shop whose back room gave onto the courtyard of the building where David worked. Other documents have him as a "caster", a "moulder" and even as a "self-employed hair-dresser"; but it is not very likely that he learned to cut hair; my mother managed the little hairdresser's shop she had leased on her own – or perhaps together with her sister Fanny.

4. It's because of this present, I think, that I've always thought frames were precious objects. Even nowadays I stop to look at them in the windows of camera shops, and I am surprised every time I come across frames for five or ten francs in Prisunic chain stores.

5. It would be fairer to say she was working towards wealth.

6. At the time this was Palestine, of course.

7. I was still strongly affected, even though already in a negative manner, by the criteria of social and economic success which made up the main part of the ideology of my adoptive family.

8. Icek is obviously Isaac and Judko is probably a diminutive of Yehudi. People might well have called my father André, just as, scarcely less arbitrarily, people called his elder brother (the one who went to seek his fortune in Palestine) Léon despite his first name being officially Eliezer. But actually everyone called my father Isie (or Izy). I am the only person to have thought, for very many years, that he was called André. One day I had a talk with my aunt about this. She thinks it was perhaps a nickname he had from his workmates or café acquaintances. For my part, I tend to think that between 1940 and 1945, when it was the most basic precaution to be called Bienfait or Beauchamp instead of Bienenfeld, Chevron instead of Chavranski, Normand instead of Nordmann, I could have been told that my father's name was André, my mother's Cécile, and that we came from Brittany.

My family name is Peretz. It is in the Bible. In Hebrew it means "hole", in Russian it means "pepper", in Hungarian (in Budapest, to be more precise) it is the word used for what in French we call "pretzel" ("pretzel" or "bretzel" is in fact merely a diminutive form [Beretzele] of Beretz, and Beretz, like Baruch or Barek, is formed from the same root as Peretz – in Arabic, if not in Hebrew, B and P are one and the same letter). The Peretzes like to think they are descended from Spanish Jews exiled by the Inquisition (the Perez are thought to be Marranos, or converted Jews

35

who stayed in Spain), whose migrations can be traced to Provence (Peiresc), then to the Papal States, and finally to central Europe, principally Poland and secondarily Romania and Bulgaria. One of the central figures of the family is the Polish Yiddish writer Isaac Leib Peretz, to whom every self-respecting Peretz is related even if it occasionally requires a feat of genealogical juggling. As for me, I am supposed to be Isaac Leib Peretz's great-great-nephew. Apparently he was my grandfather's uncle.

My grandfather was called David Peretz and lived in Lubartow. He had three children: the eldest was called Esther Chaja Perec; the second, Eliezer Peretz; and the last-born, Icek Judko Perec. In the period between the first and third births, that is to say, between 1896 and 1909, Lubartow was, in succession, Russian, then Polish, then Russian again. An official hearing in Russian and writing in Polish, it has been explained to me, will hear Peretz and write Perec. But it is not impossible that the opposite is also true: according to my aunt, the Russians are supposed to be the ones who wrote "tz", and it was the Poles who wrote "c". This explanation signals but by no means exhausts the complex fantasies, connected to the conceal-ment of my Jewish background through my patronym, which I elaborated around the name I bear, a name which is distinguished, moreover, by a minute discrepancy between the way it is spelled and the way it is pronounced in French: it should be written Pérec or Perrec (and that's how it always is written spontaneously, either with an acute accent or with a double "r"); but it is Perec, despite the fact that it is not pronounced Peurec.

9. It's obviously not my father I'm tackling here; more like a settling of old scores with my aunt.

10. I do not know the source of this memory, which nothing has ever confirmed.

11. Or rather, quite precisely on the very day, 16 June 1940, at dawn. My father was taken prisoner after being wounded in the abdomen by machine-gun fire or a shell splinter. A German officer pinned a label on to his uniform bearing the legend "Operate immediately," and he was taken into the church of Nogent-sur-Seine, Department of Aube, about sixty-five miles from Paris; the church had been converted into a hospital for prisoners of war; but it was crammed full and there was only one medical orderly on the spot. My father lost all his blood and died for France before they could operate. Messrs Julien Baude, chief inspector of taxes, aged thirty-nine years, residing at 13 Avenue Jean-Casimir-Périer, Nogent-sur-Seine, and Edmond Charles Gallée, mayor of said town, signed his death certificate at nine o'clock the same day. My father would have been thirty-one three days later.

12. It was in 1955 or in 1956. This pilgrimage lasted a whole day. I spent the entire afternoon in an empty snack bar waiting for the train to take me back to Paris. My visit to the cemetery was very short. I didn't have to search for long amongst the two or three hundred crosses in the military cemetery (just a square plot in the corner of one of the municipal graveyards). Finding my father's grave, seeing the words PEREC ICEK JUDKO followed by a regimental number, stencilled on the wooden cross and still perfectly legible, gave me a feeling that is hard to describe. The most enduring impression was that I was playing a role, acting in a private play: fifteen years after, the son

37

comes to meditate on his father's grave. But beneath the role-playing there were other things: astonishment at seeing my name on a grave (since one of the curiosities of my name has long been its uniqueness – in my family no one else is called Perec); the dreary feeling of doing something I always had had to do, that I could not possibly have never done, but which I would never know why I should do; wanting to say something, or to think of something; a muddled see-sawing between unmanageable emotion on the verge of incoherence, and indifference at the absolute limit of what can be willed; and underneath that something like a secret serenity connected to this rooting in space, to this writing on the cross, to this death which had at last ceased to be abstract (your father *is* dead, or, at school, at the start of the new school year when you have to fill in little slips for teachers you've not had before – father's occupation: deceased), as if the discovery of this tiny patch of earth had at last put a boundary around that death which I had never learnt of, never experienced or known or acknowledged, but which for years and years I had had to deduce hypocritically from the commiserating whispers and sighing kisses of the ladies.

That day I was wearing for the first time ever a pair of black shoes and an absolutely hideous dark twill suit with white pinstripes which some member of my adoptive family had had the kindness to fob off on me. I came back to Paris with mud up to my knees. The shoes and the suit were cleaned, but I found a way of ensuring that I would never wear them again.

13. I committed three spelling mistakes just in copying out this name: Szulewicz, not Schulevitz.

38

14. Thanks to this name I have always known, as it were, that Saint Cecilia is the patron saint of musicians and that the cathedral at Albi – which I didn't see until 1971 – is dedicated to her.

15. For Klajnerer, read Klajnlerer.

16. I have only heard speak of her younger sister and of two brothers, who both became cobblers, one of whom is perhaps still settled in Lyons. I think that around 1946 one of my maternal uncles came to Rue de l'Assomption – where my aunt Esther had taken me in – and spent the night there. I think that around the same time I met a man who had been in my father's regiment.

17. This can only be my aunt Fanny; it is possible that her official forename was Soura; I have forgotten from what source I obtained all these details.

18. I would not put things that way now, obviously.

19. I can't quite pin down the exact sources of this fantasy; one of them is definitely Andersen's *The Little Match Girl*; another may be the episode in *Les Misérables* where Cosette is at the Thénardiers'; but it is likely that the whole thing comes from a quite specific story.

20. In fact, Aaron – or Aron – Szulewicz, whom I knew as much or as little as I knew my other grandfather, was not a craftsman but a greengrocer.

21. This time the image alludes specifically to traditional illustrations of Tom Thumb and his brothers or alterna-

tively to Louis Jouvet's numerous children in *Bizarre Bizarre*.

22. In France my mother learned to write French, but she made a lot of mistakes; during the war my cousin Bianca gave her some lessons.

23. In fact my mother arrived in Paris, with her family, when she was still a small child, that is to say probably straight after the end of the First World War.

24. These details, like most of the preceding ones, are given completely at random. However, I still have on most of the fingers of both my hands, on the second knuckle joints, the marks of an accident I must have had when I was a few months old: apparently an earthenware hot-water bottle, which my mother made up, leaked or broke, completely scalding both my hands.

25. It was the *Compagnie industrielle de Mécanique horlogère*, better known under the name of "Jaz". My mother worked there as a machinist from 11 December 1941 to 8 December 1942.

26. There were actually a number of French edicts which were supposed to protect particular categories of people: war widows, old people, etc. I find it really hard to understand how my mother and so many others managed to believe in them even for a moment.

We never managed to find any trace of my mother or of her sister. It may be that they were deported towards Auschwitz and then diverted to another camp; it is also possible that their entire trainload was gassed on arrival.

My grandfathers were also both deported: David Peretz, they say, died of suffocation on the train; no trace of Aron Szulewicz was ever found. My paternal grandmother, Rose, owed it to chance alone to have escaped arrest: she was at a neighbour's house when the gendarmes came; she took refuge for a time in the Sacré-Cœur convent and managed to get to the free zone not, as I believed for years, by being locked up in a trunk, but by hiding in the guard's van on the train.

My mother has no grave. It was only on 13 October 1958 that she was officially declared to have died on 11 February 1943 at Drancy (France). A subsequent decree dated 17 November 1959 stipulated that "had she been of French nationality" she would have been entitled to the citation "Died for France".

★

I possess other pieces of information about my parents; I know they will not help me to say what I would like to say about them.

Fifteen years after drafting these two passages, it still seems to me that I could do no more than repeat them: whether I added true or false details of greater precision, whether I wrapped them in irony or emotion, rewrote them curtly or passionately, whether I gave free rein to my fantasies or elaborated more fictions, whether or not, moreover, I have made any advances in the practice of writing, it seems to me that I would manage nothing more than a reiteration of the same story, leading nowhere. A text about my father which I wrote in 1970, and which is rather less good than the first, is enough to convince me that I do not want to start again now.

41

It is not – as for years I claimed it was – the effect of an unending oscillation between an as-yet undiscovered language of sincerity and the subterfuges of a writing concerned exclusively with shoring up its own defences: it is bound up with the matter of writing and the written matter, with the task of writing as well as with the task of remembering.

I do not know whether I have anything to say, I know that I am saying nothing; I do not know if what I might have to say is unsaid because it is unsayable (the unsayable is not buried inside writing, it is what prompted it in the first place); I know that what I say is blank, is neutral, is a sign, once and for all, of a once-and-for-all annihilation.

That is what I am saying, that is what I am writing, and that's all there is in the words I trace and in the lines the words make and in the blanks that the gaps between the lines create: it would be quite pointless to hunt down my slips (for instance, I wrote "I committed" instead of "I made", à propos of my mistakes in copying down my mother's name), or to muse for hours on the length of my father's *capote*, or to comb my sentences for, and obviously locate straightaway, soppy little echoes of the Oedipus complex or of castration, for all I shall ever find in my very reiteration is the final refraction of a voice that is absent from writing, the scandal of their silence and of mine. I am not writing in order to say that I shall say nothing, I am not writing to say that I have nothing to say. I write: I write because we lived together, because I was one amongst them, a shadow amongst their shadows, a body close to their bodies. I write because they left in me their indelible mark, whose trace is writing. Their memory is dead in writing; writing is the memory of their death and the assertion of my life.

NINE

"And then?"

"What do you mean, 'and then'?"

"What have I got to do with this story, apart from having a namesake in it who drowns?"

"Nothing, for the time being. This is where I come into it, actually. The brief sketch of events I have given may have led you to believe that I knew the Wincklers intimately, or that I belonged to the assistance organization which made it possible for you to find, in this very place, under the cover of a new identity, a degree of safety which nothing has put in jeopardy up to now. But nothing could be further from the truth. Until fifteen months ago, or more exactly up to 9 May last year, the most likely date of the shipwreck, your story and your namesake's story were quite unknown to me. Though I am not much of a music lover, I knew that Caecilia Winckler was a great singer, and I think I even heard her sing the part of Desdemona at the Metropolitan shortly before the war. On the other hand, though I had never had any direct dealings with it or with any of its members, I knew by name the assistance organization which helped you and I was favourably disposed towards the considerable work it performed on every front. My sympathy was in a sense a professional one, and it is in a professional capacity that I involve myself today in Gaspard Winckler's story and, by repercussion, in yours – I work, you see, for a Shipwreck Victims' Relief Society. It is a private international organization funded in part by charitable bodies, in part by private donations, in part by government or municipal institutions, for

example the Ministry of the Merchant Navy, or the Union of North Sea Chambers of Commerce, and most of all by insurance companies. It began as a kind of extension of the Bureau Veritas. You don't know what the Bureau Veritas is?"

"No," I confessed.

"It is an organization which was set up in the early nineteenth century and which publishes annual statistics on shipbuilding, maritime traffic, shipwrecks and damage at sea. At the end of the last century one of the Bureau's directors expressed the wish in his will that a portion of the then very substantial subsidies paid each year to the organization by governments be allocated to relieving the victims of shipwreck, instead of to just counting them. The proposal was quite outside the scope of the Bureau's constitution, but the fashion at that time was for relief and rescue societies, and the Board of Directors therefore resolved to set aside half of one per cent of its annual budget to establish a philanthropic body responsible for collecting all the facts about vessels in distress and, in so far as its modest means permitted, for coming to their assitance. A little later, Lloyd's Register of Shipping and the American Bureau of Shipping, two of the Bureau Veritas's rival bodies, joined in this project and the Shipwreck Victims' Relief Society began to grow as best it could."

"I do not really see how you can operate; when a ship goes down, you are obviously not there on the spot!"

Otto Apfelstahl looked at me fixedly for a few seconds without speaking. I realized that the bar was deserted again; the only person left, right at the back, was a barman in a black jacket (not the one who had served me, nor one of the ones who had come later); he was lighting candles stuck in old bottles and setting them out on the tables. I looked at my watch; it was nine o'clock. Was I still called Gaspard Winckler? Or was I going to have to seek him out at the other end of the world?

"When a boat goes down," Otto Apfelstahl continued at last

44

(and his voice seemed amazingly close, and his slightest word affected me directly, as if it were me he was talking about), "then either there is another ship not too far off that comes to her assistance — which is what happens in the most favourable case — or there is not, and the passengers pile into rubber dinghies or onto whatever can be used as a raft, or they cling to spars or to the disabled wreckage and drift with the current. Most of them are swallowed up by the sea in the first three or four hours, but some kind of hope gives certain survivors the strength to live on for days, weeks even. A few years ago, one such was found more than five thousand miles away from where he had been shipwrecked, lashed to a barrel, half eaten away by seasalt, but still alive after more than three weeks in distress. You may have heard of a steward in the British merchant navy who survived on a raft for four and a half months, from 23 November 1942 to 5 April 1943, after his ship sank in the Atlantic off the Azores. Instances such as these are rare, but they do happen, just as even now shipwreck victims do get washed onto reefs or desert islands, or find a fragile refuge on an ice floe that is shrinking by the day. Our help can be given most effectively to this type of victim. Large vessels follow known routes, and rescue operations can almost always be set up very rapidly, even for serious disasters and criminal damage. Our work is focused primarily on isolated cases: yachts, small leisure craft, trawlers that go down. Thanks to a network of correspondents which is now established at all key points, we can collect all the necessary information in record time and co-ordinate rescue services. To our offices come the bottles thrown into the sea and their modern equivalents, the Maydays transmitted by sinking ships. Though our searches most often end, alas, with the discovery of corpses already half torn to shreds by sea birds, it can also happen that one of our launches or 'planes or helicopters arrives at the scene of the disaster in time to save one or two human lives."

"But did you not say a moment ago that the Sylvander *went down fifteen months ago?"*

"Yes indeed. Why do you ask me that?"

"I suppose you expect me to take part in this search?"

"Quite so," said Otto Apfelstahl. "I should like you to set off for those parts and find Gaspard Winckler."

"But why?"

"Why not?"

"No, what I meant was: what hope can you still reasonably entertain of finding a shipwreck victim after fifteen months?"

"We pinpointed the Sylvander *just eighteen hours after she transmitted her distress signals. She had broken her back on the shoals of a tiny island to the south of Isla Santa Ines, in latitude 54° 35'S by longitude 73° 14'W. Despite storm-force gales, a Chilean Civil Defence rescue team succeeded in reaching the yacht a few hours later, the following morning. Inside, they found five corpses, and they were able to identify them: Zeppo and Felipe, Angus Pilgrim, Hugh Barton and Caecilia Winckler. But there was a sixth name on the manifest, the name of a ten-year-old child, Gaspard Winckler, and his body they did not find."*

TEN

RUE VILIN

We lived in Paris, in the xxth *arrondissement*, in Rue Vilin. It's a shortish, roughly S-shaped street that leads uphill from Rue des Couronnes to some steep steps giving on to Rue du Transvaal and Rue Olivier Metra (this intersection is one of the last street-level points from which you still have a view over the whole of Paris, and it is where Bernard Queysanne and I filmed the closing shot of *Un Homme qui dort* in July 1973). Today, Rue Vilin has been three-quarters demolished. More than half the houses have been razed, leaving waste ground, piling up with rubbish, with old cookers and wrecked cars; most of the houses still standing are boarded up. A year ago my parents' old house, number 24, and the one where my maternal grandparents, and Aunt Fanny as well, used to live, number 1, were still more or less intact. At number 24, you could even see, over a boarded-up wooden door giving on to the street, a sign, still just about legible, saying: LADIES' HAIRDRESSING. I think that when I was very little the street had wooden paving. Perhaps there was even a great heap, somewhere, of nice cubic wooden paving blocks with which, like the characters in Charles Vildrac's *L'Ile rose*, we built castles and cars.

I went back to Rue Vilin for the first time in 1946, with my aunt. I think she spoke to one of my parents' neighbours. Or maybe it was simply that she had brought me to see Rose, my grandmother, who left Villard-de-Lans and came back to Rue Vilin for a while before going to live with her son Léon in Haifa. I think I can remember playing in the street for a bit. For the following fifteen years I did not have any occasion, or any wish, to go back. In those years I would not have been able to say where the street was and I would more likely have put it near Belleville or Ménilmontant metro stations than around Couronnes.

With friends who lived very near there, in Rue de l'Ermitage, I went back to Rue Vilin in 1961 or 1962, on a summer evening. The street brought back no sharp memories, only a vague awareness that it might possibly be familiar. I did not succeed in identifying the house where the Szulewiczes had lived, nor the one in which I had spent the first six years of my life and which I believed, mistakenly, to have been number 7.

Since 1969 I have been to Rue Vilin once a year in connection with a book I am writing, currently entitled *Les Lieux* ("Places"), in which I try to describe what happens over twelve years to a dozen places in Paris to which I am particularly attached for one reason or another.

The building at number 24 is made up of several modest, one- and two-storey constructions around a small and distinctly squalid courtyard. I don't know which is the part I lived in. I haven't attempted to go inside any of the dwellings, which are inhabited nowadays mostly by Portuguese and African immigrant workers, since I am in any case convinced that it would do nothing to revive my memories.

I think David, Rose, Isie, Cécile and I lived together. I

don't know how many rooms there were, but I don't believe there were more than two. Nor do I know where Rose had her grocery shop (perhaps at number 23, Rue Julien-Lacroix, which bisects the lower part of Rue Vilin). One day Esther told me that Rose and David lived in a different part of number 24 from my parents, in a concierge's office. That may simply mean it was a ground-floor room, and that it was tiny.

TWO PHOTOGRAPHS

The first was taken by Photofeder, 47 Boulevard de Belleville, Paris XI. I think it dates from 1938. It shows me and my mother in close-up. Mother and child make a picture of happiness, enhanced by the photographer's shading. I am in my mother's arms. Our temples touch. My mother's hair is dark, brushed up at the front and falling in curls over the nape of her neck. She is wearing a flower-printed bodice, perhaps held by a brooch. Her eyes are darker than mine and have a slightly wider shape. Her eyebrows are very fine and sharply delineated. Her face is oval, her cheeks well defined. My mother bares her teeth as she smiles a rather silly, uncharacteristic smile, presumably in response to the photographer's request.

I have fair hair with a very pretty forelock (of all my missing memories, that is perhaps the one I most dearly wish I had: my mother doing my hair, and making that cunning curl). I am wearing a light-coloured jacket (or sleeved vest or coatee), buttoned up to the neck, with a little quilted collar. I have big ears, puffy cheeks, a small chin, and a lopsided grin and sidelong glance which are already quite recognizable.

The second photograph has three inscriptions on the back: the first, half missing (because one day I stupidly trimmed the margins of most of these photographs), is in Esther's handwriting and can be read as: "Vincennes, 1939"; the second, in my hand, in blue ballpoint, indicates: "1939"; the third, in black pencil, hand unknown, could be "22" (most probably it is a mark made by the photographer who developed the film). It is autumn. My mother is seated or, more exactly, leaning on a kind of metal frame, the two horizontal struts of which can be seen behind her; something like a section of one of those fences made of wire and wooden posts which are commonly found in Paris parks. I am standing next to her, on her left – the right-hand side of the photograph – and her black-gloved left hand rests on my left shoulder. On the right-hand edge there is something which might be the overcoat of the person taking the photograph (my father?).

My mother wears a felt hat, wound round with a ribbon, down over her eyes. A pearl is set in her earlobe. She is smiling sweetly with her head leaning very slightly to the left. Since this photo was not retouched, as was very definitely the case with the previous one, you can see she has a big beauty spot next to her left nostril (to the right of the photograph). She is wearing a dark overcoat with wide lapels, open over a probably rayon polo-neck bodice, fastened by seven broad white buttons, the seventh barely visible, a very narrow-striped calf-length grey skirt, stockings that may be similarly grey, and rather odd welted shoes with thick crepe soles, raised vamps and thick leather laces with something like tassels at the ends.

I wear a beret and a dark raglan coat that is done up by two large leather buttons and comes down to mid-thigh, above bare knees, dark woollen socks around my ankles, and single-button bootees that may be polished.

My hands are chubby and my cheeks are plump. I have big ears, a slight sad smile, and my head leans a little to the left.

In the background there are trees that have already lost most of their leaves, and also a little girl wearing a light-coloured coat with a tiny fur collar.

BOULEVARD DELESSERT

Both my parents worked, and so did my grandmother. During the day I was looked after by Fanny. She often took me to Boulevard Delessert, where my aunt lived with her daughter Ela. I suppose we caught the metro at Couronnes, changed at Etoile, and got off at Passy. It must have been at Boulevard Delessert that Ela tried to make me ride a bicycle and my screaming roused the whole neighbourhood.

THE EXODUS

My earliest firm memories are of school. I don't think it likely I went to school before 1940, before the Exodus. Personally, I have no memory of that great flight from Paris, but I do have a photo which bears its trace. In trimming it I rendered indecipherable the notation of where it was taken, which Esther may have made and has since forgotten but the date – June 1940 – is still visible.

I am at the wheel of a toy car, which I remember as red but which here is obviously light in colour, perhaps with some red trim (air intake slats on the side of the bonnet). I have a kind of one-button jersey on, either with short sleeves or with the sleeves rolled up. My hair is uncontrollably curly. I have got big ears, a wide smile, eyes crinkling with pleasure. I am leaning my head slightly to the left (to the right in the photograph). Behind me there is a closed iron-railing gate, its bottom part reinforced with a fine wire mesh, and, right at the back, a farmyard with a cart.

I don't know where this village was. For years I believed it was in Normandy, but I rather think it was east or north of Paris. Several times in fact, there were air raids nearby. A friend of my grandmother's had fled there with her children and had taken me with her. She told my aunt that she hid me under the eiderdown each time there was a raid, and that the Germans who occupied the village liked me a lot and played with me, and that one of them spent his time giving me rides on his shoulders. She was very afraid, she said to my aunt who subsequently told me, that I might say something I shouldn't say and she didn't know how to get me to understand the secret I had to keep.

(She was a very fat and very kind woman, my aunt told me. She was a trouser machinist. Her son became a doctor. Her daughter worked as a stringer in my uncle's pearl business, then left for America, got married, and brought her mother over.)

A PHOTOGRAPH

Written on the back is "Montsouris Park 19(40)". The handwriting is a mixture of capitals and small letters: perhaps it is my mother's, which would make it the only sample of her hand that I possess (I have none of my father's). My mother is sitting on a garden chair at the edge of a lawn. In the background, trees (coniferous) and a tall succulent. My mother is wearing a big black beret. Her coat may be the same one she has on in the photograph taken at Bois de Vincennes, to judge by the button, but this time it is done up. Handbag, gloves, stockings and lace-up shoes are all black. My mother is a widow. Her face is the only light spot in the photograph. She is smiling.

SCHOOL

I have three memories of school.[1]

The first is the haziest: it takes place in the school basement. We're shoving and pushing. We're being made to try on gas masks: big isinglass goggles, a waggly bit sticking out, a sickening smell of rubber.

The second is more persistent: I am running – not exactly running: at each stride I do a hop on the foot that is forward; it's a running style, halfway between proper running and hopping, which is very common amongst children, but I don't know any specific term for it – I am running, then, down Rue des Couronnes, holding out at arm's length a drawing I did at school (a painting, actually) which depicts a brown bear on a dark-brown ground. I am drunk with excitement. I am yelling for all I am worth: "Here come the cubs! Here come the cubs!"

The third memory is, it seems, the most coherent. At school we used to get points. They were little squares of yellow or red cardboard on which was written "1 point", in a garland frame. When you got a certain number of points in a week, you could claim a medal. I wanted to get a medal and one day I got it. The teacher pinned it on to my smock. At the end of school, on the staircase, there was pushing and shoving that rebounded from step to step, from child to child. I was halfway up the stairs and I pushed a little girl over. The teacher thought I had done it on purpose; she pounced on me and without listening to my protests tore the medal from me.

I can *see* myself running down Rue des Couronnes with that specifically childish running step, but I can still physically *feel* that shove in the back, that flagrant proof of injustice; and the sensation in my whole body of a loss of balance imposed by others, coming from above and falling on to me, remains so deeply imprinted on my body that I wonder if this memory does not in fact conceal its precise opposite: not the memory of a medal torn off, but the memory of a star pinned on.

1. Virtually as I wrote up these three memories, a fourth came back to me: that of the paper place-mats we made at school: we laid out, side by side, narrow strips of thin cardboard of various colours and wove identical strips crosswise, once over, once under. I remember being delighted by this game, that I quickly understood how it worked and was very good at it.

THE DEPARTURE

My mother took me to the Gare de Lyon. I was six. She entrusted me to a Red Cross convoy leaving for Grenoble, in the free zone. She bought me a magazine, an issue of *Charlie*, with a cover showing Charlie Chaplin, with his walking stick, his hat, his shoes and his little moustache, doing a parachute jump. The parachute is attached to Charlie by his trouser braces.

The Red Cross evacuates the wounded. I was not

wounded. But I had to be evacuated. So we had to pretend I was wounded. That was why my arm was in a sling.

But my aunt is quite definite: I did not have my arm in a sling; there was no reason at all for me to have my arm in a sling. It was as a "son of father deceased", a "war orphan", that I was being evacuated by the Red Cross, entirely within regulations.

On the other hand, perhaps I had a rupture and was wearing a truss, a suspensory bandage. I think that on arrival in Grenoble I had an operation – for years I believed Professor Mondor had performed the operation, a detail I lifted from I don't know which other member of my adoptive family – for hernia and appendicitis at the same time (presumably they took advantage of the rupture to get rid of my appendix). It was definitely not straight after my arrival in Grenoble. According to Esther, it was later, and for appendicitis. According to Ela, it was for a rupture, but much earlier, in Paris, when I still had my parents.[1]

A triple theme runs through this memory: parachute, sling, truss: it suggests suspension, support, almost artificial limbs. To be, I need a prop. Sixteen years later, in 1958, when, by chance, military service briefly made a parachutist of me, I suddenly saw, in the very instant of jumping, one way of deciphering the text of this memory: I was plunged into nothingness; all the threads were broken; I fell, on my own, without any support. The parachute opened. The canopy unfurled, a fragile and firm suspense before the controlled descent.

1. Actually I was wearing a truss. I had the operation in Grenoble, a few months later, and my appendix was taken

55

out at the same time. That doesn't make any difference to the fantasy; it just allows me to track down one of its sources. As for the imaginary arm in a sling, we shall see it making a curious reappearance later on.

ELEVEN

"By checking the ship's log against harbour documents from each port of call, against weather reports and radio positioning records, we were subsequently able to make a fairly adequate reconstruction of the circumstances in which the Sylvander *went down. The yacht's last port of call was Port Stanley, in the Falklands; from there she reached Le Maire's Strait, rounded Cape Horn, and then, instead of sailing on to the Pacific, steered back up into Nassau Bay and, by way of the very narrow passage between Hoste and Navarino Islands, proceeded into Beagle Channel almost directly off Ushuaia. On 7 May, at noon, as was his daily custom, Hugh Barton took his bearings and noted the position in the log: something like latitude 55° and so many minutes s and longitude 71° w, that is to say roughly on a level with the Brecknock peninsula, the westernmost part of Tierra del Fuego proper, between O'Brien Island and Londonderry Island off the last foothills of the Darwin Mountains, or less than one hundred nautical miles from the site of the shipwreck. The next day, unusually, bearings were not taken or, in any case, not entered in the log, which from our point of view comes to the same thing. On 9 May, at three a.m., a Norwegian whaler working in the Weddell Sea and a radio ham on Tristan da Cunha picked up a distress call from the* Sylvander *but failed to establish radio contact with her. The call was relayed to us less than two hours later, but the yacht had already gone silent, and when our stations at Punta Arenas and Cape Hermit tried to raise contact it was to no avail. The report of the Chilean rescue service makes it clear that the* Sylvander's *SOS was put out very shortly, a few*

57

minutes, maybe even only twenty or thirty seconds, before the disaster. The lifeboat stays had not been unfastened, three of the five corpses were not even dressed, no one had had the time to put on a life buoy. The force of the collision was fantastic. Angus Pilgrim was literally smashed against his cabin bulkhead; Hugh Barton's skull was shattered when the mainmast fell on him, Zeppo was torn to shreds on the rocks and Felipe was decapitated by a steel hawser. But the most horrible death was Caecilia's: she did not die instantly like the others, but, with her back broken by a badly lashed cabin trunk which had come adrift in the impact, she had tried, probably for hours on end, to reach and to open her cabin door; when the Chilean rescue team found her, her heart had only just stopped beating, and her bleeding fingernails had made deep scratches in the oak door."

"And her son?"

"His cabin was next to Caecilia's. Everything in it, clothes, toys, was topsy-turvy. But he was not there."

"Perhaps he went overboard."

"That is very unlikely. He would have to have been on deck, and he had no reason to be there."

"But if he had been?"

"At three a.m.! What would he have been doing on deck at three in the morning?"

"Maybe someone, – Hugh Barton, for instance – thought that the sight of the tempest would have a real impact on the child . . ."

But Otto Apfelstahl shook his head.

"No," he said, "that is impossible. If he had been swept overboard, the sea would have smashed him on the barrier rocks, and we would have found a trace, a clue, something of his, blood, a lock of hair, a hat, a shoe, something or other. No; we looked, our frogmen dived until they were exhausted, we searched every cranny of the rocks. To no avail."

I did not speak. It was as though, at this point in his story, Otto Apfelstahl expected me to give a reply or at least a sign of some sort, even if only an expression of indifference or hostility. But I found nothing to say. He too fell silent; he was not even looking at me. Somewhere someone was playing an accordion. I had a momentary vision of a sailors' dive in some sub-Arctic port, three seamen swaddled in thick blue scarves, drinking Oxo and blowing on their fingers. I hunted in my pockets for a cigarette.

"Your packet is on the table," Otto Apfelstahl said quietly.

I took a cigarette. His hand stretched out, offering a lighter flame. I mumbled barely audible thanks.

We remained silent like that for maybe five minutes. Now and again I drew a lungful of dry and acrid smoke. Otto Apfelstahl seemed lost in contemplation of his lighter which he was turning round and round in every direction. Then he cleared his throat two or three times.

"If," he said at last, breaking an increasingly oppressive silence, "if we take into account the Sylvander's average speed, and her noon position as calculated and logged on 7 May, then we can see that at three a.m. on 9 May she should have been much further west. If, moreover, we accept that a master will fail to perform the elementary but essential safety routine of taking his daily bearing only in the event of extreme disruption or something close to outright panic, then we are led of necessity to only one conclusion. Can you see what it is?"

"I think so, but I am not sure there is only one."

"What do you mean?"

"They turned around to look for him: that could mean the boy had escaped — maybe he had — but it could also mean they had abandoned him and then had had a change of heart."

"Does that make any difference?"

"I do not know."

Another long silence ensued.

"How did you track me down?" I asked.

"I was somewhat fascinated by this catastrophe, by the victims' personalities, by the kind of mystery surrounding the boy's disappearance. From port of call to port of call I reconstructed the story of the voyage: I contacted the families and friends of those lost, obtained sight of the letters they had received. Three months ago, taking advantage of a trip to Geneva, I met Caecilia's former private secretary, a man you know, the one who gave you your identity papers; he told me of your existence, told me what he knew of your story. You were much easier to find than the other one. There are only twenty-five Swiss consulates in the whole of Germany . . ."

"And more than a thousand islands in Tierra del Fuego," I added, thinking aloud.

"Yes, over a thousand. Most of them are inaccessible, uninhabited, uninhabitable. The Argentinian and Chilean Coast Guard have searched the others, tirelessly."

I said nothing. For a brief moment I wanted to ask Otto Apfelstahl if he thought I would have better luck than the Coast Guard. But that was a question which from then on only I should be able to answer . . .

(. . .)

PART TWO

This mindless mist where shadows swirl
– is this then my future?

RAYMOND QUENEAU

TWELVE

Far away, at the other end of the earth, there is an island told of. Its name is W.

It lies from east to west, about nine miles long at its maximum extent. Its overall shape is something like a sheep's head with its lower jaw distinctly out of joint.

    The lost voyager, the unfortunate or self-willed victim of a shipwreck, or the bold explorer cast by fate, by the spirit of adventure or by the pursuit of some illusory quest amongst the myriad islets that dot the waters off the disjointed tip of the South American mainland would have but a poor chance of alighting on W. Indeed, its shores offer no natural landing stage, but only shallows with treacherous, barely submerged reefs, or straight, steep, unfaulted basalt cliffs, or again, to the west, in the area corresponding to the back of the sheep's head, plague-infested swamps. These swamps are fed by two warm-water rivers, called the Omeg and the Chald, whose almost parallel courses delineate for a short stretch in the heartland of the isle a fertile and verdant micromesopotamia. The profoundly hostile nature of the lands all around it – a craggy, tortured, arid, glacial landscape, perpetually shrouded in fog – makes the sight of this cool and happy countryside seem all the more miraculous: in place of barren moors swept by wild Antarctic winds, in place of splintered rock faces and meagre seaweed with millions of sea birds circling overhead, you see gently rolling hills crowned with clumps of oaks and plane trees, dusty tracks edged with dry-stone walls or high bramble hedges, and great fields of bilberries, turnips, corn and sweet potatoes.

Despite this remarkable mild climate, neither Fuegians nor Patagonians settled on W. As is still the case today for most of the other islands in these parts, W was entirely uninhabited when it was colonized, at the end of the nineteenth century, by the group whose descendants constitute the entire current population of the island. The fog, the reefs and the swamps had made it unapproachable; explorers and geographers had failed to complete or, even more often, had not begun a survey of its coastline, and on most maps W did not appear at all or featured only as a vague and nameless blob with scarcely determined distinctions between land and sea.

According to tradition, the founding and the very name of the island go back to someone called Wilson. Though this starting point is agreed upon by all, numerous variations are put forward. In one version, for instance, Wilson was a lighthouse keeper whose negligence is supposed to have caused a frightful disaster; another version has him as the leader of a group of convicts who mutinied during transportation to Australia; and in yet another, he was a disenchanted Captain Nemo who dreamt of building an Ideal City. A fourth variation, quite close to the last but with a significant difference, makes Wilson a champion (some say a trainer) excited by the idea of the Olympics: but as the difficulties which Pierre de Coubertin had to face at that time depressed him and left him convinced that the Olympic ideal could only be thwarted, sullied and distorted by sordid trade-offs and compromised unacceptably by the very people who claimed to serve it, Wilson decided to do all that was humanly possible to found a new Olympia far removed from nationalistic squabbles and ideological manoeuvres.

The particulars of these traditions are not known, and their authenticity is far from being guaranteed. That does not matter a great deal. Clever speculative interpretations of certain customs

*(for instance, particular privileges granted to particular villages),
or of some of the patronyms that are still current, could throw
some detailed light on the history of W, on the origins of its
colonizers (it is at least clear that they were white, Western,
and moreover, almost exclusively Aryan: Dutchmen, Germans,
Scandinavians, scions of that proud class called WASPs in the
United States), on how many they were, on the laws they
established, etc. But it doesn't make much difference whether W
was founded by outlaws or by sportsmen. What is true, what is
certain, what is immediately striking, is that W, today, is a land
where Sport is king, a nation of athletes where Sport and life
unite in a single magnificent effort. The proud motto*

FORTIUS ALTIUS CITIUS

*emblazoned on the monumental arches at the gates of each village,
the splendid stadiums with their meticulously maintained cinder
tracks, the gigantic wall sheets which publicize the results of
sporting contests hour by hour, the celebrations held daily for the
winners, the men's dress: grey tracksuits with an outsize W
emblazoned on the back, such are the sights which greet the newly
arrived visitor. From them, he will grasp with wonderment and
enthusiasm (for who would not become enthusiastic on sight of
that bold discipline, those daily achievements, those neck-and-neck
struggles, the intoxication of victory?), that life, here, is lived for
the greater glory of the Body. And it will later be seen how the
athletic vocation shapes the life of the State, how Sport rules W,
how it has fashioned social relations and individual aspirations
through and through.*

THIRTEEN

From this point on, there are memories – fleeting, persistent, trivial, burdensome – but there is nothing that binds them together. They are like that unjoined-up writing, made of separate letters unable to forge themselves into a word, which was my writing up to the age of seventeen or eighteen, or like the dissociated, dislocated drawings whose scattered elements almost never managed to connect up and with which, at the time of "W", roughly, that is, between my eleventh and fifteenth year, I filled whole exercise books: human figures unrelated to the ground which was supposed to support them, ships with sails that did not touch the masts and masts which did not fit into the hulls, machines of war, engines of death, flying machines and implausible mechanical vehicles with disconnected nozzles, discontinuous cordage, disengaged wheels rotating in the void; the wings of the planes were detached from their fuselages, the legs of the athletes were separated from their trunks, their arms were out of their torsos, their hands gave them no grasp.

What marks this period especially is the absence of landmarks: these memories are scraps of life snatched from the void. No mooring. Nothing to anchor them or hold them down. Almost no way of ratifying them. No sequence in time, except as I have reconstructed it arbitrarily over the years: time went by. There were seasons. There was skiing and haymaking. No beginning, no end. There was no past, and for very many years there was no future either; things simply went on. You were there. It happened somewhere far away, but no one could have said very precisely where it was far from, maybe it was just far from Villard-de-Lans. From time to time you changed places, went to another boarding house or another family. Things and places had no name, or several; the people had no faces. One time it was an aunt, next time it was another aunt. Or a grand-mother. One day you met your cousin and you had almost forgotten you had a cousin. After that you didn't meet anyone; you didn't know if that was normal or not normal, if things were going to be like that all the time, or if that was just a passing phase. Maybe there were auntie times and no-auntie times? You didn't ask for anything, you didn't really know what you should ask for, you must have been a bit afraid of the answer you'd get if you did make up your mind to ask for something. You didn't ask any questions. You waited for fate to bring auntie back, or if not that aunt, then the other – in the end you didn't much care which one it was and anyway you didn't really care whether there were any aunties at all or not. It was still a bit of a surprise, in fact, that there were any aunties or cousins; or a grandmother. You could get by in life quite well without, you couldn't really see the point, nor why these people were more important than the others; it wasn't very nice, the way aunties appeared and disappeared any old time.

The only thing you do know is that it went on for years and then one day it stopped.

Even my aunt and my cousins have forgotten a great deal. My aunt remembers that she used to look at the Alps; she used to wonder why the small farm she could see on the edge of the forest wasn't her grandfather's; she could have been born there; she would have spent all her childhood years playing there.

As for me, I would have liked to help my mother clear the dinner from the kitchen table. There would have been a blue, small-checked oilcloth on the table, and above it, a counterpoise lamp with a shade shaped almost like a plate, made of white porcelain or enamelled tin, and a pulley system with pear-shaped weights. Then I'd have fetched my satchel, got out my book and my writing pad and my wooden pencil-box. I'd have put them on the table and done my homework. That's what happened in the books I read at school.

FOURTEEN

Most of the population of W is concentrated in four settlements simply called "villages": there is W village, certainly the oldest, which was founded by the first generation of W-men, and North-W, West-W, and North-West-W villages, situated respectively to the north, west and north-west of W. The villages are sufficiently close to allow a runner leaving his own village at dawn to get round the three others and return to his point of departure by lunchtime. This is in fact a very popular exercise, and many sports managers use it as a prelude to training sessions, not only for long-distance runners but for all athletes, including throwers, jumpers and wrestlers.

The road connecting the villages is particularly narrow and the custom was quickly established of performing this morning exercise one way round – specifically, in a clockwise direction. It is obviously a serious infringement of the rule to run the wrong way. In so far as the notion of sin is, on W, if not totally unknown, then at least fully integrated into a sports morality (any fault, intentional or unwitting – a meaningless distinction on W – leads to automatic disqualification, in other words to defeat, a penalty of huge, not to say capital, importance), failure to respect a custom unconnected with competition can only be meant as a challenge: on this very simple basis, quite complex machinery has been built to govern intervillage events.

In order to understand the machinery, which is one of the main pillars of W life, the concept of "village" has to be gone into in rather more detail. It is not the entire population which lives in the villages, but only the sportsmen, together with those people who, though they no longer perform in any sport or take part in any contests, are directly necessary to the sportsmen: team managers, trainers, doctors, masseurs, dieticians, etc. People whose jobs relate not to the individual contestants but to their contests – namely, in descending order of rank and responsibility, organizers, race managers, judges and referees, timekeepers, guards, musicians, torchbearers, standard bearers, dovekeepers, track sweepers, servers, etc. – are housed in the stadiums or their outbuildings. All others whose jobs do not or do not any longer relate directly to Sport, that is, mainly, the old men, the women and the children, are accommodated in a set of buildings located a few miles south-west of W in a place called the Fortress. That is where, amongst other things, the central hospital and sick bay, the asylum, the youth homes, the kitchens, workshops, etc., are located. The name of the Fortress derives from its central building, a crenellated and almost windowless tower made of soft grey stone, a kind of petrified lava, which could quite easily remind you of a lighthouse. The tower serves as the seat of the Central Government of W. It is where the major decisions are taken, in the greatest secrecy, on matters concerning, in particular, the organization of the biggest sports meetings, the Games, of which there are three: the Olympiads, the Spartakiads, and the Atlantiads. Members of Government are selected from amongst Organizers and from the corps of Judges & Referees, but never from amongst Athletes. The running of a sports state does in effect require total impartiality, and any Athlete, however honest he might otherwise be, and however great his sense of fair play, would be too tempted to favour his own victory or, failing that, a victory for his own camp, to be able to respect the implacable neutrality required of the Judges. More generally, no administrative function at any level is ever entrusted to a practising Athlete. Villages and stadiums (in some sense the municipal tiers of the Government) are run by officials appointed by Central Authority: usually timekeepers and race managers (by "race manager" is meant a low-ranking organizer responsible for the proper conduct of a single event, not to be confused with "sports manager" or "team manager" responsible for training Athletes and keeping them in shape).

To sum up, on W, a village is roughly the equivalent of what might be called elsewhere an "Olympic village", of what in Olympia itself was called the Leonidaion or, alternatively, of the training camps where sportsmen of one or more nations limber up before major international events.

Apart from the Athletes' accommodation, each village is equipped with training circuits, a gymnasium, a swimming pool, a massage parlour, a sick bay, etc. Halfway between each village and its neighbour is a stadium of modest size used only for contests between those two villages. Roughly in the middle of the quadrilateral formed by the four villages is the Central Stadium, a far more imposing structure, which is the venue for Games, that is to say, contests between representatives of all the villages, and for what are called "selection trials" or just "selections" for short, that is to say, contests between non-adjacent villages. It is clear that W, for instance, can have daily matches with North-W (in the stadium they share at the midpoint between W and North-W) and with West-W (in the stadium midway between W and West-W) but has little opportunity to measure its strength against North-West-W since there is no stadium which the two share directly. Similarly, North-W has few chances of meeting West-W. The rates of meeting between the different villages are therefore quite variable. As often happens, these differences have exacerbated rivalries between villages: out of a kind of "villager" reflex, the Athletes end up regarding their opponents in the village not adjacent to theirs as their worst enemies. Consequently, contests between non-proximate villages are characterized by a fighting

73

spirit, an aggressiveness and a thirst for victory which give them an appeal sometimes lacking in meetings between adjacent villages and, a fortiori, in ranking heats within a single village.

As can be seen, competitions are of four kinds. At the bottom of the ladder are the heats in which Athletes of a given village win the right to take part in intervillage meetings.

Next come the local championships between proximate villages; they are four in number: W vs North-W, W vs West-W, North-W vs North-West-W, West-W vs North-West-W.

Then come the "selections" which set non-adjacent villages against each other: W vs North-West-W and North-W vs West-W.

And finally there are the Games which, as we have said, are three in number: the Olympiads, held once a year; the Spartakiads, held every three months and which are, by way of exception, open to Athletes who are not ranked in their own villages; and the Atlantiads, held once a month.

The dates of Games are laid down by Central Government. Other meetings are governed by the rules of challenge: every morning, at the start of the limbering-up circuit, an Athlete from one of the villages who has been selected the previous evening by his sports manager sets off the wrong way round and challenges the first Athlete he meets. There are three possibilities: the challenged Athlete may be from the Athlete's own camp, in which case that day's contest will be the internal village heats: or he may be from one of the two adjacent villages, which means local championships; or he is from a non-proximate village, and there will be a selection trial.

FIFTEEN

Henri, my father's sister's husband's sister's son whom I have since become accustomed to calling my cousin although he is no more my cousin than his mother Berthe was my aunt, or Marc my uncle, or Nicha and Paul my cousins, had asthma, and, from before the war, he had been recommended the middle-altitude mountain air of Villard-de-Lans. That is the reason why all the members of my adoptive family who had not decided to emigrate to the United States – about two-thirds of them, in fact – together with some of their connections (by which I mean distant relatives) and friends, along with a fairly large number of people, generally but not compulsorily Jewish, from all corners of Occupied France and sometimes from even further afield, from Belgium for instance, took refuge at Villard-de-Lans and filled the villas, family hotels and children's homes with which, fortunately, Villard was bountifully supplied.

My aunt Esther lived with her family in a fairly secluded villa right at the top of the main road which comes down the hill to the main square of Villard, and lower down turns into one of the two principal streets of the village, at least as far as shops are concerned. The Gardes' farmhouse, where Marc, my uncle David's brother, lived with his wife Ada and their children Nicha and Paul, was also off this road, on the downhill side, on the right, and further up on the left was a villa called the Igloo, where Berthe, David's sister, lived with her husband, Robert, and their son, Henri.

I think I knew what an igloo was: a shelter made by Eskimos from blocks of ice piled on top of each other; but I probably didn't know the meaning of the word "frimas" (rime) which was the designation of aunt Esther's villa. Until this very moment, when, out of an autobiographer's belated scruple I have been impelled to look it up in various dictionaries, I went on believing the explanation I was probably given the first time I asked what the word meant: I thought it was a poetic expression for winter, with connotations of white snow as well as of harsh weather and I have only just learnt – and am wondering how I managed not to know for so long – that it denotes quite specifically freezing fog.

I have no precise memory of the house itself, though I passed by it again not so long ago, in September 1970. I know it has an outside staircase, with a solid balustrade supporting big stone spheres, because three of the spheres are visible on a photograph that portrays a group of teen-agers standing on the stairs on a summer's day; my cousin Ela and my cousin Paul can be made out amongst them.

Near the house, on the other side of the road, there was a farm – today it's a factory making plastic knick-knacks – where there lived an old man with grey whiskers. He wore collarless shirts (the collarless shirts Orson Welles liked to make Akim Tamiroff wear, the ones that always make me think of the lost dignity of displaced persons or the humbled pride of grand dukes reduced to shoe-shining) and I remember him clearly: he sawed his wood on a saw-horse made of a pair of up-ended parallel crosses, each in the shape of an X (called a "Saint Andrew's Cross" in French), connected by a perpendicular crossbar, the whole device being called, quite simply, an x.

My memory is not a memory of the scene, but a memory of the word, only a memory of the letter that has turned into a word, of that noun which is unique in the language in being made of a single letter, unique also in being the only one to have the same shape as the thing it refers to (the draftsman's T-square is called a Té in French, pronounced like the letter it resembles, but its name is not written "T"), but it is also the sign of a word deleted (the string of x's crossing out the word you didn't mean to write), the contrastive sign of ablation (as in neurophysiology, where, for example, Borison and McCarthy [*J.appl. Physiol.* 34 (1973): 1 – 7] compare intact cats [*intact*] with cats with an excised vagus [VAGX] or carotid [CSNX]), the sign of multiplication and of sorting (the x-axis), the sign of the mathematical unknown, and, finally, the starting point for a geometrical fantasy, whose basic figure is the double V, and whose complex convolutions trace out the major symbols of the story of my childhood: two Vs joined tip to tip make the shape of an X; by extending the branches of the X by perpendicular segments of equal length, you obtain a swastika (卐), which itself can be easily decomposed, by a rotation of 90 degrees of one of its 〉 segments on its lower arm, into the sign 〉〉; placing two pairs of Vs head to tail produces a figure (XX) whose branches only need to be joined horizontally to make a star of David (✡). In the same line of thinking, I remember being struck by the fact that Charlie Chaplin, in *The Great Dictator*, replaced the swastika with a figure that was identical, in terms of its segments, having the shape of a pair of overlapping Xs (✖).

★

Behind the villa there was a large rock with a face that was pretty well unclimbable – I think I remember seeing one of my pseudo-cousins, probably Nicha, making a victorious ascent – but fairly easy to get at from behind, the only difficulty being a "chimney" offering no convenient crannies and which had to be climbed by putting your weight on to your shoulders, your backside and the palms of your hands on one wall, and using your feet, on the other wall, to lever you up. The pride I must have felt on accomplishing this modest feat probably explains why it has been preserved for posterity. I am posing (one foot slightly forward, hands behind my back) on the top of the rock; the perspective effect of the ground-angle shot is barely noticeable, and from this one can only draw the obvious inference that this great rock was of utterly middling height.

My hair is cut very short, I am wearing a light-coloured, short-sleeved shirt and darker shorts of rather odd design: they don't appear to have flies, and button up at the side; it could well be a pair belonging to my cousin Ela; what's more, they are too big for me, not so much in length (I've checked on other photographs – of Henri and of Paul, amongst others – that at that time short trousers easily went down to the knee) as in breadth, which emphasizes the length of the belt that is holding them in at the waist; my legs are bare and very tanned; there may be a suggestion of knock-knees (apparently I was very rickety when I got to Villard, but that can hardly be seen on the photograph); I am wearing white sandals which must have been made of real or synthetic rubber; I am looking straight at the lens, my mouth half-open in a semi-smile; my ears are gigantic and stick out prominently.

★

I don't think I lived at Les Frimas for very long, perhaps only for a few weeks subsequent to my arrival at Villard at the end of spring 1942. I remember that my uncle had a very beautiful racing bicycle, which Ela sometimes used, and on which he could make the return trip to Grenoble in a single day, which I thought an amazing feat. I also remember my aunt making pasta by spreading the dough right out over a flour-dusted wooden tabletop and using a knife to cut it into long thin strips which were then put out to dry. Another time she went so far as to make soap from a mixture of soda and beef dripping (and perhaps also even ash).

★

Though chronologically impossible, since it could only have occurred in the real winter, and in spite of later evidence that it never happened at all, I persist in situating in this first short period the following scene: my aunt and I are going down the road to the village; on the way, my aunt meets a lady with whom she is friendly and whom I greet, putting out my left hand to shake hers: a few days earlier, whilst skating on the ice rink at the bottom of the ski run called Les Bains, I had been knocked over by a sledge; I fell backwards and broke my scapula; it is a bone that cannot be set in plaster; to allow it to mend, my right arm has been strapped tight behind my back in a whole contraption of bandages that makes any movement impossible, and the right sleeve of my jacket flaps emptily as if I really had lost an arm.

Neither my aunt nor my cousin Ela have any memory of this fracture, which, as it aroused universal sympathy, afforded me ineffable delight.

In December 1970, I went to spend a few days with a

friend who lives at Lans, four miles from Villard, and there I met a builder called Louis Argoud-Puix. Born and brought up at Villard, he was about my age, and we had no trouble recalling a mutual friend, Philippe Gardes, whose parents had housed Marc, Ada, Nicha and Paul for many months, and whose elder sister later married Nicha. During my last year at Villard I went to the village school with Philippe. Louis Argoud-Puix told me that he had been in the same class as Philippe throughout his school years, but he did not remember me at all. I asked him if he remembered the accident I was supposed to have had. He didn't remember that either, but he was greatly surprised to hear of it, because he did have a precise recollection of an accident identical in every way – in its causes (ice-skating, sledge impact, backward fall, broken shoulder blade) as in its consequences (no plaster-setting possible, the use of a tight bandage which made it look as though an arm had been lost) – which had happened to the self-same Philippe, at a date which he was unable, moreover, to specify.

The thing happened, a little later or a little earlier, and I was not its heroic victim but just a witness. As in the case of my arm-in-a-sling at the Gare de Lyon, I can see perfectly well what it was that these easily mendable fractures, which could be remedied simply by keeping them still for a stretch, were meant to stand in for, although today it seems to me that the metaphor will not serve as a way of describing what had been broken – and what it was surely pointless hoping to contain within the guise of an imaginary limb. In simpler terms, these fantasy treatments, more like supports than like straitjackets, these *marks of suspension* indicated pains that could be named; they cropped up on cue to justify an indulgence the actual cause of which was mentioned only in an undertone. Whatever the truth of the matter, and as far back as I can remember, the word "scapula" and its companion, the word "clavicle", have always been familiar to me.

SIXTEEN

After various trials and errors which reflected the friction between the traditionalists who wished to maintain only the events of the classical Games, or, at most, the twelve selected for the 1896 Athens Games, and the modernists who wished to introduce other disciplines, such as weight-lifting, gymnastics or football, Games Administration ended by deciding upon twenty-two events to be contested.

Apart from Graeco-Roman wrestling (which, here, is actually a kind of pancratium in which the wrestlers, besides fighting with their bare hands, are allowed to hit each other with their elbows which are padded with lead-lined leather), all twenty-two events fall in the domain of track and field athletics. Twelve of them are running events, including three sprint contests (100 metres, 200 metres, 400 metres), two at middle distances (800 and 1,500 metres), three at long distances (5,000 metres, 10,000 metres, marathon), three over hurdles (110 metres, 200 metres, 400 metres), and the 3,000-metre steeplechase event; seven are contests, including three in jumping (high jump, long jump, hop-skip-and-jump) and four in throwing (putting the shot, throwing the hammer, the discus, and the javelin). Alongside these nineteen athletics events there are two mixed competitions involving several disciplines, the pentathlon and the decathlon. Quite inexplicably, but perhaps for reasons of physique, pole-vaulting is not, or is no longer, contested. Nor are there any relay races; here they would have no meaning, would not be understood by spectators: an individual win is always a win for the team, so a "team win" means nothing.

For the Games to hold their interest, there obviously has to be keen rivalry between the representatives of the villages. Every village is thus required to have contestants on the starting line for every race and therefore has to train its men with this requirement in mind. Consequently the training of Athletes is highly specialized, and for each type of event, the villages try to produce men who will be the best in that event, and only in that one.

The complement of Athletes in each village fluctuates between 380 and 420. This is made up of a variable number (between 50 and 70) of novices (fourteen-year-old boys from the Youth Homes who fill places in the villages as they are vacated by veterans) and an immutable number of competitors: 330 divided into 22 teams of 15 Athletes each. When an Athlete leaves his team, either because he has reached the age limit or because he appears incapable of further satisfactory performance or as the result of an accident, then the Sports Managers choose from among the senior novices (by then seventeen or eighteen years old) the one who, on the basis of physique, physiological and psychological traits, and results in training, seems most suited to take his place.

The ranking heats held regularly in each village for each team allow the best three of the fifteen Athletes to be identified. These three seeded Athletes are the ones who represent the village in the local championships, in the selection trials and in the Olympiads. The best two win, in addition, the fiercely prized right to take part in the Atlantiads. On the other hand, it is the last twelve – that is to say, the unseeded Athletes – who enter the Spartakiads.

This so to speak dynastic distribution can be seen largely as the expression of a concern for organization: it allows a precise and exhaustive tally of Athletes to be kept, which, from the Officials' point of view, reduces checking procedures to a minimum. It is an established fact that in the whole of W there are sixty 100-metre sprinters in four teams of fifteen, of whom six run in the local championships and selection trials, eight run in the Atlantiads, twelve in the Olympiads, and forty-eight in the Spartakiads. It is similarly settled that there are 176 contenders in the Atlantiads, 264 in the Olympiads and 1,056 in the Spartakiads. Once established, these numbers quickly became immutable and were incorporated into the rituals of the eliminating heats. Thanks to these numbers, meetings of all kinds proceed with absolute regularity, which is something that Games Administration, with its constant concern for efficiency, can only applaud.

Clearly, for Sports Managers, whether they are in charge of a whole village or only of a team, the system has its disadvantages. The most serious is that it rules out multiple winners. As is well known – the results of most Olympics, including Thorpe's double gold at Stockholm, Hill's two wins at Antwerp, Kuts's at Melbourne, Snell's at Tokyo, Zatopek's hat-trick at Helsinki, Owens's at Berlin, and the four golds taken by Paavo Nurmi at Paris, are there to prove it – a sprinter is usually as good at the 100 metres as he is at the 200 metres, a middle-distance runner is usually as strong in the 800 as in the 1,500 metres, and a long-distance man generally performs as well in the 5,000 metres, the 10,000 metres and the marathon. Thus most Sports Managers facing a major contest would often be strongly disposed to put the same Athlete – whichever one was currently in top form – on the starting line in several different events. Although that is theoretically possible, and though no written law formally prohibits multiple entries, it is simply unheard of: no village has ever dared enter fewer than the expected number of contestants in a meeting, presumably for fear of displeasing the Organizers, if only because the Athletes are presented to the Officials – at the opening of the Olympiads, for example – in the shape of a huge W made by the 264 competitors, and a scaled-down team (relying on one of its champions to win several events) would spoil the perfection of this human mosaic.

People prefer to say, whatever the facts of the matter, that training methods are sufficiently well geared to the different types of event that one sprinter, for example, can be prepared specifically for the 100 metres whilst another is trained up for the 200 metres.

That obviously leaves the case of the pentathlon and the decathlon. One of the consequences of such ultra-specialized training is that there is no time – and, to tell the truth, no method either – for training an Athlete to perform with basic competence in five or ten different events. The multi-sport training programme followed by novices in their first few years in the villages would be the least inappropriate, but the half-hearted attempts to continue it at professional level, pursued with a view to producing genuinely broad-ranging Athletes, were not crowned with success. That is easily explained: the laws of sport on W, as every village quickly realized, are such that it is better to concentrate on winning five events with five Athletes each trained simply for his own event, than to put everything into a single event with a sole Athlete required to be victorious in five or ten contests.

The Organizers were initially amazed at the utterly deplorable performances in the decathlon and the pentathlon, and at one time they came close to abolishing these events. In the end they retained them, but with completely new features which adapted them to the mediocre level of the contestants: they turned them into joke events, mock contests intended to give the spectators some relief from the very great tension that reigns during most of the competition: the pentathlon and decathlon contestants enter the stadium dressed as clowns, wearing outrageous make-up, and each event is used as a pretext for mockery: the 200 metres is run three-legged, the 1,500 metres is a sack race, the take-off board in the long jump is often dangerously slippery, etc. Winning these events certainly requires some athletic talent, but above all it takes acting ability,

85

a certain sense of mime, of parody and of the grotesque. A novice who pulls faces, or suffers from a tic, or has a slight handicap (he may be rickety, for instance, or have a limp or be slightly lame, or he may display some tendency to obesity or on the contrary be extremely thin, or have a bad squint) runs a real risk – but there are far greater risks to incur than those of being sacrificed to the derision of a crowd – of being put into the pentathlon or decathlon team.

That is also where a serving Athlete excluded from his event may end up – making it one of the very rare instances of changing team – if he has been dropped because of an accident, for example, whilst too young to enjoy veterans' rights and is clearly unsuited to becoming a trainer, and if he has the right backing.

SEVENTEEN

The children's home where I was first sent as a boarder was run by a man called Monsieur Pfister (he was perhaps a Swiss). Louis Argoud-Puix is sure that this home was called Le Clos-Margot, though in my vague and distant memory it bears a bird's name (for instance, Les Mésanges, "The Tits"). Apparently, according to my aunt, I couldn't tie my own laces yet; that may have been one of the requirements for being accepted as a boarder (like being able to cut your own meat, turn taps on and off, drink without spilling, not wet your bed, etc).

The house was close by Les Frimas and during this time, which lasted, I think, only a few months, I must have had frequent contact with my foster family. That is how I can remember going one day with my aunt Esther to see her sister-in-law Berthe at the Igloo; they sat in the lounge and Berthe sent me upstairs to play with her son Henri, who must have been twelve or thirteen. I don't know why I have such a precise memory of the staircase: it was very narrow and steeply raked. I found Henri and a distant cousin of his by the name of Robert (Henri's aunt was the wife of Robert's maternal grandfather's cousin, or vice versa) sitting on the floor playing furiously at running battleships (a rather complicated version of battleships in which, as you might guess, the ships are allowed to move during play; I shall be mentioning this game again); they refused from the start to let me join in, saying I was too small to understand the mechanics of it, which I found very humiliating.

★

I knew nothing of the outside world except that there was a war, and that, because of the war, there were refugees: one of these refugees was called Normand and lived in a room in a house that belonged to a man called Breton. That's the first joke I can remember.

There were also Italian soldiers, the Alpine light infantry, in uniforms, I think, of garish green. They weren't much in evidence. They were said to be stupid and harmless.

EIGHTEEN

It is clear that the overall organization of sporting life on W (the villages, the way teams are made up, selection methods, to mention only the basic elements) has as its sole aim to heighten competitiveness or, to put it another way, to glorify victory. In this respect it can indeed be said that no other human society can rival W. The survival of the fittest is the law of this land; yet the struggle itself is nothing, for it is not Sport for Sport's sake, achievement for the sake of achievement, which motivates the men of W, but thirst for victory, victory at any price. Just as the spectators in the stadiums do not forgive an Athlete for losing, neither do they spare their applause for the winners. All hail to the victorious! Woe betide the vanquished! For the village citizens, professional sportsmen all, nothing but victory is conceivable – victory at every level: against their own team mates, in inter- village meetings, and finally, above all, in the Games.

Like all the other moral values of the society of W, the glorification of success has a concrete expression in daily life: grandiose ceremonies are held in honour of victorious Athletes. True, in all ages victors have been celebrated: they have gone up on to the podium, had their country's national anthem played, been awarded medals, statues, cups, certificates, crowns, have been made freeman of their native towns, been decorated by their governments. But such celebrations and honours are as nothing beside what the Nation of W accords to its deserving. Every evening, irrespective of the type of contest held that day, the first three in each event mount the podium, are clapped and cheered at length by the crowd, have bouquets, confetti, handkerchiefs thrown at them, receive from the hands of the Official Calligraphers the emblazoned certificate recording their achievement, and are granted the great privilege of raising their village's standard to the top of the Olympic flag pole; the three leaders from each event are then led in procession behind torchbearers, standard bearers, dove-keepers and trumpeters to the great halls of the Central Stadium where a ritual reception awaits them in all its splendour and bounty. They strip off their tracksuits and are offered a choice of magnificent apparel, from embroidered costumes to silk capes with scarlet frogging, spangled uniforms glittering with decorations, evening dress, and doublets with lace ruffs and trim. They are presented to the Officials, who raise their glasses and drink a toast in their honour. Wild rounds of toasts and libations ensue. The Athletes are given a banquet which often goes on till dawn: the most exquisite dishes are placed before them, accompanied by the headiest of wines, the most succulent cold meats, the suavest of sweets, the most intoxicating spirits.

The celebration feasts at the big Games are obviously more copious and splendid than the feasts held for the winners of ranking heats or local championships. But that difference, however marked, is not essential to an understanding of the value system which prevails on W. What is much more significant, on the other hand, and constitutes one of the singular features of W society, is not that the losers are excluded from the festivities – that is only fair – but that they are purely and simply denied their evening meal. It goes without saying, clearly enough, that if victors and vanquished alike were both to have food, then the only privilege for the winners would be that their food was of better quality, banquet fare in place of everyday nourishment. The Organizers, not without reason, considered that perhaps that would not suffice to give contestants the fighting spirit needed for top-level competitions. In order to win, an Athlete has to have the will to win.

A concern for personal standing, the desire to make a name for oneself, national pride, can all no doubt function as powerful motives. But at the crucial moment, at the point where a man must give his best, where he must surpass his own strength and find, somewhere outside of himself, that extra ounce of energy which will enable him to snatch victory, it is quite useful if what is at stake effectively partakes of a basic survival mechanism, almost an instinctive self-protection: what the Athlete grasps in winning is much more than the necessarily ephemeral glory of having been the best; it is — by the sole fact of his obtaining an extra meal — a guarantee of better physical condition, an assurance of a better-balanced diet and, consequently, of better form.

It can now be appreciated how subtly the dietary system of W supports the overall social system, to an extent that makes it one of the main articulations of social structure. Naturally the absence of an evening meal does not in itself constitute a mortal deprivation. If that were the case, then sporting life, and life itself, would have come to an end long ago on W: indeed, simple arithmetic shows that in the best instance, namely the ranking heats, only 264 Athletes, out of a total of 1,320, have a chance of eating dinner. After local championships or selection trials, the number falls to 132, and at the end of Games only 66 remain — that is to say, quite precisely, one in twenty. The vast majority of Athletes would therefore be chronically undernourished. But they are not: their diet includes three meals a day, the first very early in the morning, before the cross-country warm-up, the second at noon, after training sessions are finished, the third at 4 p.m., during the traditional half-time between the eliminating heats and the finals. On the other hand, these meals are carefully designed to fulfil the athletes' dietary and caloric needs only in part. Their sugar content is virtually nil, as is the quantity of vitamin B1, essential for the assimilation of carbohydrates. Athletes are thus subjected to a consistently deficient intake which in the long run seriously undermines their resistance to muscle fatigue. From this point of view, victors' banquets, with their fresh fruit, sweet wines, dried bananas, dates, strawberry preserves, compotes and chocolate tablets, therefore constitute a veritable carbohydrate compensation indispensable for the Athletes' physical health.

The problem with this method is obviously the risk that, by giving an advantage to the winners and harshly penalizing the losers in an area directly related to the physiological basis of the contest, it will emphasize the differences between the contestants and produce in the end a kind of vicious circle: the winners of the day, rewarded that very evening with additional sugar rations, have every chance of winning again the following day, and so on, with the one group becoming ever more sturdy, the other ever weaker. That would of course deprive the contests of all interest, since the results, so to speak, would be known in advance. The Organizers have taken no particular steps to remedy this problem. Instead of forbidding victors to enter the stadium on the day after they win – a provision that would obviously be contrary to the whole spirit of W – they have preferred (and in so doing have once again shown their wisdom and their profound understanding of the human heart) to put their trust in what they call, laughingly, nature. Experience has proved them right. The winners are not debarred from the next day's contests. But more often than not they have spent the night carousing, and only returned to quarters in time for reveille. Sugar-starved, they usually bolt their food, stuff themselves like pigs. Dizzy with victory, they let themselves go and reply to every toast drunk in their honour, mixing wines and liqueurs until they are under the table. It is easy to understand why, in these circumstances, Athletes almost never win twice in a row. Prudence would suggest that the winners ought to hold back, that they should refrain from drinking or at least limit themselves, and take food selectively and with moderation. But the temptations are so great for the feted prizewinners that it *would take an uncommonly tough character to resist them. And besides, restraint is not encouraged: neither by the Officials — who, quite the contrary, are constantly inviting them to drain their glasses — nor by the Sports Managers, who, with their concern for the well-being of their teams, have every interest in a speedy turn-over of winners, so as to ensure, as regularly as possible and for the greatest possible number of their Athletes, the essential energizing sustenance provided by these evening meals.*

NINETEEN

Collège Turenne, which was also called the Belltower, was quite a large, pinkish building, probably not very old, situated a little outside Villard, maybe five hundred yards beyond Les Frimas, as I discovered with amazement when I returned to visit it in December 1970, so firmly did I remember it as a frightfully far off place where no one ever went, a place which news never reached, whence those who crossed its threshold never returned.

The school was a religious foundation run by two sisters (perhaps in the ordinary as well as the religious sense of the word) whom I imagine, rather than remember, in long grey robes, with huge bunches of keys on their waistbands. They were strict and not much given to showing affection. The tutor, on the other hand, was a man of great kindness, and for him I had feelings that were close to veneration; he was called Father David, he was a Franciscan or Dominican friar, dressed in a white robe with a belt of plaited string at the end of which hung a rosary. Whatever the weather, he went barefoot but for sandals. I think I remember he was bald and had a big red beard. According to my aunt, he was a converted Jew, and it was perhaps as much out of proselytizing zeal as out of concern for my protection that he insisted I be baptized.

I do not know how my religious education proceeded and I have forgotten every bit of the catechism that was drummed into me, except that I tackled it with exaggerated keenness and piety. In any case I still have an extremely detailed memory of my baptism, which was performed sometime in the summer of 1943. That morning I made a vow of poverty – that is to say, I decided that, as a first step, I would wear my everyday clothes at the ceremony. I had withdrawn to a corner of the kitchen garden at the back of the school and was deep in my prayers when the headmistresses and two cleaning women came upon me. They had been looking for me for an hour. They grabbed hold of me and, disregarding my protests, undressed me, soaked me in a tub of cold water, and rubbed me down untenderly with household soap (or whatever substitute was used in those days) before forcing me into a magnificent sailor suit. My only consolation was that I could keep my own shoes, which had nothing ceremonial about them.

The sailor suit belonged to my godfather, a Belgian boy who had escaped to Villard with his sister, who was my godmother. They were, I was later told, the children of one of the Queen of Belgium's ladies-in-waiting. It was probably they who gave me, as a baptism present, a kind of picture in relief of the Virgin and Child in a gilded frame, which I contemplated piously all afternoon at the back of the classroom, having been excused exercises, and which that evening I hung over my bed.

Next morning I handed back the suit, but my piety and faith remained exemplary and Father David made me religious prefect of my dormitory and entrusted me with giving the signal for evening prayers and with making sure they were properly executed. On some days I received permission to rise before the others and to attend the Mass which Father David, assisted by a single altar-boy, said for himself and the two headmistresses in the little chapel with its stylized Stations of the Cross, whose tower had given the school its nickname. My dearest wish would have been to be that altar-boy, but this was not possible: before that I had to make my First Communion, then my solemn Communion, and even be confirmed. I knew the seven sacraments, and Confirmation seemed to me to be the most mysterious of all, perhaps because it takes place only once (unlike Communion – or Eucharist – and Confession – or Penance – which can at a pinch be a daily event) and because its profound uselessness (why bother to confirm what Baptism has already pronounced?) is associated with a ritual which involves a real dignitary of the Church, a bishop. A bishop was an official person, a personality, a personage of quasi-historical dimensions for me; as yet I knew of no equivalent, since I paid no attention to generals – whom eighteen months or two years later I was to start idolizing – or to ministers, or to sporting champions, who, it must be said, had scarcely any opportunity to shine in those troubled times.

A bishop came to the school to confirm some of the boarders, probably amongst the eldest, with a slap, which seemed all the more symbolic for being absolutely dissimilar to what I knew as a smack, a wallop, or a cuff. The ceremony was as fabulous as I had been told, and was held in the open; to my grave disappointment, the bishop did not wear his mitre or carry his crozier; he wore a black habit with only a purple stole and hood to indicate his great eminence. I remember I very much wanted to touch him, but I don't know if I succeeded.

I have a vague memory of the litanies, a weak impression of still being able to hear the endless reiteration of the "Ora pro nobis" echoed in chorus after each saint's name. To this memory is attached the remembrance of punning rounds in which a number sequence leads, usually fairly soon, to a play on words: "I one a rat, I two a rat, I three a rat, I four a rat, I five a rat, I six a rat, I seven a rat, I ate a rat", and also: "What one? What two? What three? What four?"

I also remember "I am a Christian, wherein lie my glory, my hope and my succour" but of course I've forgotten what comes next, just as I no longer know what comes after "Unto us a boy is born, unto us a child is given . . ."

TWENTY

From the very founding of W it was decided that the names of the first victors should be maintained piously in men's memories and be attached to all their successors on the podium. The custom took root at the second Olympiads: the winner of the 100 metres was given the title of Jones, the 200 metres champion was dubbed MacMillan, and the 400 metres, 800 metres, marathon, 110 metres hurdles, long jump and high jump medallists were entitled, respectively, Gustafson, Müller, Schollaert, Kekkonen, Hauptmann and Andrews.

The custom spread quickly and the same system was soon used for designating the winners first of the Spartakiads and selection trials and then of the local championships and ranking heats. In the end, the runners-up who, to begin with, were distinguished by the adjunction of the honorifics "silver" and "bronze" to their names, were likewise accorded titles which were the names of the first-time winners of their places in their respective events.

It was quite obvious that it would not be long before these titles, as proudly flaunted as medals, as symbols of victory, would become more important than the Athletes' names. Why say of a winner: "His name is Martin, he is the Olympic 1,500 metres champion" or: "His name is Lewis, he came second in the triple jump in the W vs West-W locals," when all you need to say is: "He is the Schreiber," or: "He is Van den Bergh." The discarding of proper names was entirely within the logic of W: Athletes' identities were soon indistinguishable from the catalogue of their performances. On this simple foundation – an Athlete is no more and no less than his victories – was built an onomastic system as subtle as it was precise.

Novices have no names. They are called "novice". They are distinguished by having sewn onto the backs of their tracksuits not a W, but a large triangle of white material, the apex pointing down.

Practising Athletes have no names, they have nicknames. Initially the nicknames were chosen by the Athletes themselves; they referred to distinctive features (Skinny, Broken Nose, Harelip, Gingernut, Curly), or to character traits (Crafty, Hothead, Plodder), or to ethnic or regional origins (the Frisian, the Sudeten, the Islander). Subsequently, almost totally arbitrary denominations were added on, deriving from Red Indian naming systems no doubt by way of their Boy Scout imitations: Buffalo Heart, Fleetfoot Jaguar, etc.

The Administration has never looked kindly on the existence of these nicknames which, being very popular amongst the Athletes, jeopardise the status of title names. Not only has it always refused to recognize nicknames (officially an Athlete is designated – apart from the names he may have gained by his victories – only by the initial letter of his village, followed by a serial number), it has managed, on the one hand, to restrict their use to home villages, thus avoiding the risk of their popularity spreading through the stadiums, and, on the other hand, to forbid the introduction of any new ones. The nicknames are now hereditary: an Athlete leaving his team bequeaths his official name (that it is to say his serial number in the village) as well as his nickname to the novice who takes his place. For a time people smiled on seeing a huge chap dubbed "Weed" or an overweight man answering to the name of "Tiny". But by the third generation these nicknames had lost all force of meaning. Thenceforth they were but neutral markers, barely more human than the official registration numbers. All that counted then were the names gained from winning.

The way Athletes are ranked and competitions organized means that there are fewer names than Athletes (which is only obvious, since names indicate victories) and that one Athlete – and this is a signal feature of the W naming system – can bear several names.

From the ranking heats come 264 names, 66 for each village, corresponding to the three front runners in each of the 22 events contested. The four local championships provide four times 66 more, that is to say, another 264; and the two selection trials supply a further two times 66, or 132. The Olympiads and Spartakiads each have 66 victors, or another 132 names. Lastly, the Atlantiads, which consist of a quite special kind of race, have an indeterminate number of winners (usually 50 to 80), all entitled to the same name – to wit, Casanova. Thus the total number of names on all of W is 793. But since local championships, Selections, Olympiads and Atlantiads are all contested by the winners of the ranking heats, it follows that the 264 seeded Athletes, who already possess names by virtue of their victories in the ranking heats, are running for 463 of the 529 titles remaining, whilst the 1,056 unseeded Athletes have only the 66 names at stake in the Spartakiads to share between them. The end result is that out of 1,320 practising Athletes only 330 will be entitled to an official identity – 264 thanks to ranking heats and other contests, and 66 thanks to the Spartakiads. The 66 Spartakiad winners will be able to bear only the titles won in those games; the others, on the contrary, will be able to combine as many as six names. Thus a 400 metres runner from North-W can concurrently

- be Westerman, by coming first in the North-W ranking heat;
- be Pfister, by coming second in the W vs North-W local championship;
- be Cummings, by coming second in the North-W vs North-West-W local championship;

- be Grunelius, by winning the North-W vs West-W selection trial;
- gain the prestigious title of Gustafson by carrying off the Olympic trophy (for Olympic winners, as for prima donnas, the definite article precedes the name thus: "the Gustafson",
- "the Jones", 'the Kekkonen" etc.
- and, lastly, be Casanova, by being placed amongst the winners of an Atlantiad.

These are the six names entered on his role of honour which would make up his official title and which he would pronounce as follows in strict and immutable order of precedence, when required to appear before the Officials: the Gustafson of Grunelius of Pfister of Cummings of Westerman–Casanova.

It goes without saying that these designations, however official they may be, are of variable duration. The Olympic champions' titles are amongst the stablest, since there is only one Olympiad a year; the title of Casanova is at stake every month, at each Atlantiad; titles deriving from victories in selections, local championships and ranking heats have to be defended almost weekly.

The title of Olympic Champion, the most enduring and by the same token the most coveted, represents a pinnacle in an Athlete's career. The custom soon arose of allowing the privilege to be retained by anyone who had won the title once, even if he never again repeated his feat. Just as a man who has been president of the Council of Ministers, even if only for a week, is addressed as "Monsieur le Président" to the end of his days, so he who wins the 110 metres hurdles in the Olympiads, even if only once, shall be called "the Kekkonen" for life. However, so as not to mistake this, or these (since there are several) honorific Kekkonens with the reigning Kekkonen, the title is slightly modified, usually by reduplicating the initial syllable. Thus: the Kekekkonen, the Jojones, the MacMacMillan, the Schoschollaert, the Anandrews, indicate the former Olympic winners in the 110 metres hurdles, the 100 metres, the 200 metres, etc.

These additional honorifics are much more than mere marks of respect. It is in fact the custom that various privileges are attached to the names. Seeded Athletes (that is to say, those who have at least one name) are entitled to move freely around the Central Stadium. Those with double names (for instance, Amstel–Jojones, third in the North-West-W 100 metres, former Olympic champion) are entitled to extra showers. Those with triple names (for instance, Moreau-Pfister-Casanova, second in the W 400 metres, second in the W vs North-W 400 metres, Atlantiad winner) are entitled to a personal trainer, called the Oberschrittmacher – that is to say Chief Trainer – no doubt because the first one to hold the post was a German; those with quadruple names are entitled to a new tracksuit, etc.

TWENTY-ONE

Once, the Germans came to the school. It was one morning. From very far away we saw two of them – officers – crossing the yard with one of the headmistresses. We went to lessons as usual and didn't see them again. At lunchtime the rumour spread that they had only looked at the school register and then, before leaving, requisitioned the pig that the cook was raising (I remember the pig: it was huge; it was fed solely on peelings).

Another time my aunt Esther came to see me. Our photograph was taken. On the back of the print is written, in whose handwriting I do not know, "1943". In the background the Alps can be seen, as well as bits of forest, fields, a hamlet and a big white chalet with a steeply pitched, flat-topped roof (a "Swiss gable" according to various dictionaries) typical of Alpine dwellings. Seven individuals – four belonging to different animal species, three to the human species – figure in the foreground. They are, from right to left (on the photograph): a) a black nanny goat with white spots, partly cut off by the right-hand margin of the photograph; it has a very long beard; it is probably tethered to a post and does not seem to realize it is being photographed; b) my aunt; she is wearing grey woollen trousers, with very narrow turn-ups and well-pressed creases, a light bodice (or blouse) with short or rolled-up sleeves, an angora wool cardigan over her shoulders, secured only by the top button. She does not seem to be wearing any jewellery. Her hair is parted in the middle, smoothly brushed back. She smiles slightly sadly, and holds in her arms c) a black-headed white kid which does not appear particularly overjoyed and is looking to the right, towards the nanny goat which is probably its mother; d) myself; with my left hand I am holding on to one of the kid's legs and with my right I hold out, as if to show its inside to the person photographing us, a large white linen or straw hat, probably my aunt's; I am wearing dark worsted short trousers, a "cowboy" check shirt with short sleeves (probably one of those I shall mention again later) and a sleeveless jumper. My socks are round my ankles; my stomach is a bit distended. My hair is cut very short, but stray locks come down onto my forehead. My ears are big and stick out; I tip my head forward a bit and stare up at the camera with a slightly dim-witted look. Distinctly to the left and to the rear of the group consisting of my aunt, the kid and myself are e) a white hen, half-hidden by f) a peasant woman of perhaps sixty wearing a long black dress and a large straw hat which obscures her face almost entirely: she has one hand on her hip; beside her is g) a horse with a rather dark coat, harnessed, blinkered, cut off midway by the left-hand margin of the photograph. Right at the bottom of the snap, on the right, can just be seen a bag made of synthetic or poor-quality leather, with large handles, which may have been my aunt's.

Another time, I think it was when we were haymaking together with masses of other children, someone came running to tell me my aunt was there. I ran towards a dark-dressed silhouette moving towards us across the field, coming from the school. I stopped short a few yards from her: I did not know the lady standing in front of me and saying hello with a smile. It was my aunt Berthe. Later I lived with her for almost a year. Perhaps during that time she reminded me of this visit, or perhaps it is an entirely imaginary event, but all the same I have an absolutely vivid memory not of the whole scene but of the sense of disbelief, hostility and mistrust which I felt at that point; even today it is not easy to express it, as if it were the revelation of a basic "truth" (henceforth only strange women will come unto you; you will seek them for ever and for ever reject them; they will not be yours, you will not be theirs, for you will be able only to hold them at arm's length . . .) the intricacies of which I don't think I have quite unravelled yet.

★

For us haymaking consisted largely in piling up a few forkloads and then sliding or somersaulting down whilst the stack was still not too high. The story was told of a little girl who had had an accident: she had jumped off the top of a haystack and landed on a pitchfork hidden in the hay; one of the prongs had gone straight through her thigh.

Another time we went gathering bilberries. I have retained a bucolic vision of a host of children on all fours spread across a whole hillside. We used a tool called a "comb", a kind of tiny wooden bucket with a serrated bottom edge, which scooped up, at each scrape, sprays laden with half-squashed berries, making a sort of blackish gunge with which we were soon covered from top to toe.

All winter long, and even longer, we skied. Every year thereafter, until the mid-fifties when I abandoned "winter sports" altogether, I was very much at ease on skis, and, without bothering about style or lessons, but with gay abandon, carefree and fast, I whizzed down any medium-hard piste and even, on occasions, coped with really perilous descents. I remember even beginning to learn to ski-jump on tiny humps of beaten snow.

The use of skis provided me with a substantial learning experience, mostly during the two years spent at Collège Turenne, and which was the source of a wealth of now otiose knowledge, the details of which, nonetheless, remain remarkably fresh in my mind. Thus I know that the finest skis are made of hickory, a Canadian wood which I went on believing to be one of the rarest substances in the world (but the scarcity of hickory was one of the proofs of its existence, whilst other things which were simply absent made you wonder how they could possibly exist: oranges, for instance – what is round and sweet and has no rhyme? . . . – which I shall mention again later, or chocolates with soft centres, or, again, even more, silver paper, in twists or in crinkly cases, wrapping up the self-same chocolates . . .). Similarly, I know that the correct length of skis is determined in the following way: when you stand upright with arms and hands stretched straight up, the top of the ski tip, standing on end, should come to the middle of the palm of your hand. To find the right length for ski-sticks, hold them with your elbows in at the waist and your forearms up; the ends of the sticks should just touch the ground. I could go on with more examples, about how to pack down the snow (the school group would get in line with their skis at right angles to the gradient and then climb up in sideways jumps), about how to wax (various grades of wax, distinguished by the colour of their cardboard packaging: blue for powdery, green for normal snow, red for schussing, white for cross-country, etc.; warm the wax before applying; to undercoat, wipe over with a stick of clear paraffin; scrape off old wax, do not let the central runnel get clogged, keep wax off the edges, which on the contrary should be sharpened, etc.), about how to get up slopes (at a time when "ski lifts" were exceptional: sideways climbing, packing down, traverse climbing, straight-up climbing, either with straight skis – with sealskins on – or herringbone fashion, with your skis making a V shape and your sticks taking your weight behind you, etc.), or about gear and tackle (the importance of having the right boots; keep them waxed; if dubbin can't be had, rub them down with newspaper crumpled into a ball; trousers and anoraks, ear-muffs, balaclavas or leather helmets, goggles, etc.), and, lastly and above all, about bindings: my skis had ankle-high bindings; they were hard to snap closed (you had to lever them with the metal spike of a ski-stick), they hardly gripped your foot, and the things would pop open all the time; I dreamt of having rostrum bindings with a lever well forward from the boot and a metal cable fitting into a groove in the heel, making the shape of a spearhead, or, even more, of that amazingly complex lacing system, the very top of the range, reserved for semi-professional skiers (and I was mightily surprised when one day I saw my cousin Ela using it), which involved the use of a single but inordinately long thong threaded over and under the boot innumerable times in an apparently unalterable routine, the execution of which seemed to me to be a cardinal ceremony (as cardinal, and as decisive, as the lacing of the Matador's belt in Blasco Ibañez's *Blood and Sand* later seemed to me to be, or the sartorial transformation of Barberini into Urban VIII in the Berliner Ensemble's production of *Galileo*), and giving the skier that indissoluble union of ski and boot which increased to the same degree the risk of a serious fracture and the chance of an outstanding performance.

We used to stack our skis in a long, narrow, concrete corridor equipped with wooden racks (I saw it again, unaltered, in 1970). One day one of my skis slipped from my hand and accidentally grazed the face of the boy putting his skis away next to me and he, in a mad fury, picked up one of his ski-sticks and hit me with it on the face, with the spike end, cutting open my upper lip. I suppose he also broke one or two of my teeth (they were still only milk teeth, but it didn't help the growth of the others). The scar that resulted from this attack is still perfectly visible today. For reasons that have not been properly elucidated, this scar seems to have been of cardinal importance for me: it became a personal mark, a distinguishing feature (though it is not entered as a "distinguishing mark" on my identity card, only on my army passbook, and I think that's only because I bothered to point it out): it is perhaps not because of this scar that I wear a beard, but it is probably so as not to hide it that I do not wear a moustache (quite unlike one of my oldest schoolmates – whom I haven't seen for over twenty years – who suffered, and that is the right word here, from a lip mark which he judged to be too distinguishing – it was, I think, not a scar but more likely a wart – and who let his moustache grow very early so as to hide it); it is this scar, also, which gave me a particular preference, out of all the paintings housed in the Louvre, or more exactly out of those in the so-called Seven-Metre Gallery, for Antonello da Messina's *Portrait of a Man Known as Il Condottiere*, which became the central figure in the first more or less complete novel I managed to write: at first it was called "Gaspard pas mort", then "Le Condottiere"; in the final version the hero, Gaspard Winckler, is a brilliant forger who can't manage to fake an Antonello da Messina and, as a result, ends up murdering the man who commissioned it from him. The Condottiere and his scar also played a preponderant role in *Un Homme qui dort* (e.g., on p. 105: " . . . the unbelievably energetic portrait of a Renaissance man with a tiny scar above his upper lip, on the left, that is to say his left, your right . . .") and even in the film that Bernard Queysanne and I made of it in 1973, the sole actor, Jacques Spiesser, having on his upper lip a scar almost identical to mine: it was pure coincidence, but it was, for me, secretly, a determining factor.

TWENTY-TWO

The rules of Sport are harsh and life on W makes them harsher still. The privileges awarded to the victors in every field are counterbalanced by an almost excessive measure of humiliation and bullying inflicted on the losers. It can go as far as physical injury, as in this theoretically prohibited custom, to which the Administration nonetheless turns a blind eye since the stadium spectators are very keen on it, whereby the man who comes last in a series has to run an extra lap with his shoes on back to front; such an exercise may seem inoffensive enough at first sight but it is in fact extremely painful, and its consequences (bruised toes, blisters, ulcers on the instep, heel and sole) destroy any hope the victim might have had of securing a respectable place in the following days' contests.

The more the winners are rewarded, the more the losers are punished, as if the good fortune of the former were the exact reciprocal of the latters' misfortune. In routine races – ranking heats, local championships – the celebrations are meagre and the penalties virtually harmless: some jeering, some booing, a bit of inconsequential ragging, nothing really any worse than the sort of forfeits losers pay in parlour games. But the greater the importance of the contest, the greater the stakes on both sides: the triumphal celebration laid on for an Olympic winner, and most specially for the winner of the race of races, that is to say the 100 metres sprint, may result in the death of the man who comes last. This outcome is both unpredictable and inexorable. If the Gods are for him, if no one in the Stadium shows a clenched fist with the thumb pointed down, he will probably save his skin and undergo only the same punishment as the other losers: like them, he will have to strip naked and run the gauntlet of Judges armed with sticks and crops; like them, he will be put in the stocks, then paraded around the villages with a heavy, nail-studded, wooden yoke on his neck. But if one single spectator rises and points to him, calling down upon him the punishment meted out to the cowardly, then he will be put to death; the whole crowd will stone him, and his dismembered corpse will be displayed for three days in the villages, suspended on the butcher's hooks which hang on the main gates beneath the five entwined circles, beneath the proud motto of W – *FORTIUS ALTIUS CITIUS* – before being thrown to the dogs.

Such deaths are rare. If they were made commoner they would lose virtually all their impact. They are customary for the Olympic 100 metres, unusual for all other events and all other contests. Of course it may happen that the stadium audience, having placed all its hopes in an Athlete, is particularly disappointed by his mediocre performance and lets fly at him, usually with a shower of pebbles or various other objects, bits of scrap iron, broken bottles, some of which can turn out to be quite dangerous. But most of the time the Organizers are against such physical assaults, and intervene to protect the lives of threatened Athletes.

However, the unequal treatment of winners and losers is far from being the only example of the systematic injustice in life on W. What constitutes the uniqueness of W, what gives its contests their special excitement and makes them unlike any others, is, specifically, that the impartiality of the results declared, of which the Judges, the Referees and the Timekeepers, in that order, are the implacable guarantors, is based on organized injustice: it is based on a fundamental and elementary inequity which, from the start, discriminates amongst the contestants in a way which tends to prove decisive.

Institutional discrimination derives from a deliberate and strictly implemented policy. If the dominant impression made by the sight of a race is one of total injustice, that is because the Officials are not opposed to injustice. On the contrary, they believe it to be the most effective stimulus, that an Athlete who is sickened by arbitrary decisions, by aberrant umpiring, by abuses of power, by the liberties taken and the almost outrageous partiality constantly displayed by the Judges, will be a hundred times more aggressive than an Athlete who is convinced that he deserved to lose.

It is necessary that even the best be uncertain of winning; it is necessary that even the feeblest be uncertain of losing. Both must take an equal risk and must entertain the same insane hope of winning, the same unspeakable terror of losing.

The implementation of this bold policy has produced a whole set of discriminatory measures which can be divided roughly into two main groups. The first kind, which could be called official measures, are announced at the start of each meeting; they usually consist of positive or negative handicaps imposed on individual Athletes, on teams, or occasionally even on whole villages. For instance, at a meeting of W and North-West-W (i.e. a selection trial), the W 400 metre team (Hogarth, Moreau and Perkins) may have to run 420 metres, whilst the North-West-W team (Friedrich, Russell, DeSouza) will finish in 380 metres. Or alternatively, in the Spartakiads, to take another example, all West-W competitors will be given a five-point penalty. Or again, the third North-W shot-putter (Shanzer) will get an extra put.

The second type of measure is unpredictable; it is left to the whim of the Organizers and, in particular, the Race Managers. The spectators can also be involved, though to a much lesser degree. The general idea is to introduce a disruptive element into a race or contest which serves either to counteract the effects of the initial handicaps or to intensify them. In this spirit, the hurdles are sometimes set slightly back for one of the runners, which puts him off his stride pattern and forces him to slow down, with an often disastrous effect on his performance. Or again, when a race is in full swing, a deceptive Referee may sometimes shout "STOP": the competitors must then stand stock still, freeze, usually in an unbearable posture, and the one who holds still longest will probably be declared the winner.

TWENTY-THREE

One afternoon in spring or summer 1944 we went on a forest walk, taking our afternoon snack or, rather, what we had probably been told were afternoon snacks, in our satchels. We got to a clearing where a group of partisans awaited us. We gave them our satchels. I remember being very proud to grasp that the meeting had not happened by chance and that our usual Thursday walk had this time been cover for getting supplies to the Resistance. I think there was a dozen of them; there must have been about thirty of us children. Obviously they were adults in my eyes, but I suppose now that they couldn't have been much over twenty. Most were bearded. Only some had weapons; one in particular had grenades; they were hanging from his braces, and that is the detail that struck me the most. Today I know they were defensive grenades, which are used for protection in a retreat, with machined steel casings which shatter into hundreds of deadly splinters, and not assault grenades, which are thrown forward before an attack and which cause more fright and racket than harm. I don't remember whether this walk was unique or whether there were several others like it. Years later I learnt that the headmistresses of the Collège Turenne were "in the Resistance".

I have a much clearer recollection of another walk, of an afternoon, shortly before Christmas, very definitely in

1943. There were far fewer of us, perhaps only half a dozen, and I think I was the only child (I was tired on the way back, and the gym teacher carried me on his shoulders). We had gone to the woods to get our Christmas tree. This was when I learnt that pines and firs were quite different trees, that what I called a fir was really a pine, that real Christmas trees were firs but there were no firs at Villard-de-Lans or anywhere in Dauphiné. Firs were taller, straighter and much darker trees than pines; you wouldn't find any this side of the Vosges. So we chopped down a pine, or rather the top of a pine with a lower trunk that was completely bare. I think that we had in our group, apart from the gym teacher, the cook and the school caretaker, who was a kind of odd-job man; it was probably he who played forester: he clipped huge semicircular crampons on to his climbing boots and clambered right up the tree with the help of a leather strap, with loops for his wrists, pulled tight around the back of the trunk (much later, when I was around twelve or thirteen, I saw an almost identical technique used again, this time by a linesman hoisting himself to the top of a telephone pole).

In the afternoon of Christmas Eve, we set up the tree in the great tiled entrance hall of the school. We decorated it and hid the wooden supports which kept it upright with moss and a kind of dark brown paper made to look like a rockery, and which was also used for the bed of the crib. I remember the treasures: stars, wreaths, candles and balls (the rest of the year they slumbered in the attic of the school) but the balls of those years were not, as they now are, spheres of very thin glass with a very shiny coating of silver paint, but balls made of a kind of papier mâché painted in mostly rather dull colours.

That evening, perhaps after Midnight Mass, but in any case, as I recall, very late, we played a prank on the gym teacher, who, like all of us, had put his shoes beneath the tree (a massive pair of ski boots which could be receptacles only for a stupendous present); we stuffed one of his boots with a gigantic parcel made of wrapping upon wrapping and containing, as its sole and ultimate gift, a carrot.

I went to bed. I was alone in my dormitory. Towards the middle of the night I woke up. I don't think the question that was racking me related directly to Father Christmas, but I was impatient to know whether I really had been given a present.

I got out of bed, opened the door silently, and went barefoot down the corridor leading to the gallery which ran round all four sides of the great hall. I leaned on the balustrade (it was almost as high as I was; in 1970, when I went to see the school again, I tried to repeat the same movement and was astonished to find that the balustrade only came to my waist). I think the whole scene has lodged and been frozen in my mind: a petrified image, unchangeable, which I can recall physically, down to the feeling of my hands clenched round the uprights, down to the cold metal pressing on my forehead when I leaned against the handrail. I looked down: there wasn't much light, but after a minute I could make out the great decorated tree, the mound of shoes all around, and, sticking out of one of mine, a big rectangular box.

It was a present my aunt Esther had sent for me: two check shirts, cowboy style. They made me itch. I did not like them.

TWENTY-FOUR

As you begin to acquaint yourself with W life, as a novice, for instance, who has moved from the Youth Homes to one of the four villages at the age of fourteen, you soon grasp that one, and perhaps the main, feature of the world that is your world from now on is that its institutions are harsh and inflexible to an extent matched only by the vast scope of the rule-bending that goes on in them. This realization, which is one of the things which determine a newcomer's personal safety, is consistently borne out, at all levels, at every moment. The Law is implacable, but the Law is unpredictable. The Law must be known by all, but the Law cannot be known. Between those who live under its sway and those who pronounce it stands an insurmountable barrier. The Athlete must know that nothing is certain; he must expect anything, the best outcome or the worst. Decisions concerning him, whether they be trivial or vital, are taken without reference to him; he has no control over them. He may well believe that his task, as a sportsman, is to win, since what is celebrated is winning, and losing is what is punished; but he may come last, and still be declared the Winner: someone, somewhere, decided that that race, on that day, would be run that way.

Athletes would be mistaken, nonetheless, were they to speculate overmuch on decisions taken in respect of them. In the majority of races and contests, the winners are indeed the best, the ones who come first, and it is almost always the case that it is advantageous to win. The rules are bent to remind Athletes that Victory is a grace and not a right: certainty is not a sporting virtue; being the best is not enough to guarantee a win, that would make it too simple. You have to know that chance is also one of the rules. The outcome of a contest may be arrived at, on some occasions, by counting out "Eeny meeny miney mo", "one potato, two potato", or any old rhyme. It is more important to be lucky than to be deserving.

The desire to "give everyone a chance" may seem paradoxical in a world where nearly everything is based on a knock-out system (the ranking heats) which in almost all cases prevents four out of every five Athletes from taking part in the main contests. Nonetheless it obviously lies at the root of two of the most typical institutions of W sports life: the Spartakiads and the Challenge System.

As we know, the Spartakiads are games open to "nameless" Athletes, who are not seeded in their own villages and who therefore do not compete in local championships or selection trials or Olympiads or Atlantiads. There are four of them a year, one each quarter. They are hotly contested meetings and the standard of competition is high, despite the fact that they set against each other the teams' weakest members, the men who, in spectators' slang, are called the "footsloggers", the "Cattleshed" or the "Nignogs". Indeed, the Spartakiads are the only chance these Athletes have of getting a name and obtaining some of the perks (shower entitlement, Stadium passes, vouchers for gear) restricted to named Athletes. Besides, the Spartakiads are contested by 1,056 Athletes, whilst only 264 take part in Olympiads, and the size of the field often makes for an exceptionally competitive atmosphere, rendering the races and contests, from heats to finals, uncommonly vigorous, and giving the whole occasion a moderately electric air; moreover the rewards are often on a par with the excitement, and the Victories of the unseeded are celebrated with a heated enthusiasm not always granted to Olympic winners.

Spartakiad winners, for the whole of the three months following their success, fully dispose of their name and the prerogatives attached to it; they are entitled, in particular, to a favourable handicap in ranking heats and it is pretty well the rule that a Spartakiad winner (a Newman, Taylor or Lömö for the 200 metres for example) will also triumph in the next ranking heat following, and will thenceforth be a full participant in all the other meetings.

Seeded Athletes obviously have nothing but scorn for the Spartakiads and their winners. It soon occurred to the Officials to use this scorn and to turn it into the driving force of a curious procedure; from it the Challenge System was born. The principle of the Challenge is simple: a seeded Athlete, who by that token has not taken part in the Spartakiad, goes up to the Winner in the minute following his victory and challenges him to repeat his achievement. In spectators' slang, he is said to be "quoining" or "posing" him. The Spartakist is not allowed to decline; at best he may hope to beat his challenger thanks to the sometimes substantial handicap allowed by the Judges, and to be determined by the Race Managers, less in relation to the Winner's fatigue than to the standard of the "quoiner"; in principle, the more famous the quoiner (the more names he has), the greater the handicap is. So if the Jones of Humphrey of Arlington von Kramer–Casanova (those names denoting the 100 metres sprinter who came second in North-West-W, Olympic Winner, etc.) challenges Smolett Jr (Winner of the Spartakiad 100 metres), Smolett Jr starts thirty metres ahead, which over such a short distance probably constitutes a decisive advantage. If the Jones beats him all the same, he will immediately take over the other's Victory and rake in not only his name (Smolett Jr) but also the names of the men who came second (Anthony) and third (Gunther) in the race, which, in theory, ensures him substantial privileges. If on the other hand he loses, what he loses is his most coveted title, *the title of the Jones, his Olympic Winner's title, to be worn from that point on, together with all its related prerogatives, by the Smolett Jr (now the Jones of Smolett Jr) whom he had so rashly challenged.*

The Challenge System is an outstanding example of a double-edged sword. For just as the Spartakist cannot decline the challenge, so no seeded Athlete may refuse to proffer it to him, once the crowd or an Official has made the request. The Officials' mood, as they set the handicap that the challenger concedes to the one challenged, is all that determines the outcome of the contest: either it will deprive the Spartakist of the only Victory he could hope to carry off, or else it will dethrone in an instant an Athlete grown insolent from all his Victories. It's not that the Officials are all that opposed to insolence; on the contrary, they often encourage it, they find it entertaining. They like their Winners to be Gods to the stands, but they are not averse, as at a stroke they despatch into the Hell of the nameless men who, a moment before, believed they had escaped from it for ever, they are not averse to reminding everyone that Sport is a school of modesty.

TWENTY-FIVE

Several times, as on that Christmas Eve, I was alone, or at least the only child, in the Collège Turenne. I explored every bit of it. Once, one summer afternoon, I opened a door that led up to the attic: it was a long corridor under the slope of the roof, where daylight came in through narrow dormer windows, and which was filled with cases and trunks. In one of the trunks, perhaps beside the Christmas-tree decorations I mentioned previously, I came upon rolls of celluloid, probably educational films or films for religious instruction, which I unwound and looked at against the light. Most of them were of no interest to me and I put them back as carefully as I could. One of them showed the desert, with palm trees, oases, camels; I kept a big piece of that one and never tired of looking at it.

At the start of the next term I invented a rather curious scheme: I told all my classmates that next year I would be going to Palestine, and showed them the strip of film as if it were proof that I was not lying. The ploy was not entirely gratuitous; it was intended as a way of obtaining portions of the snacks my classmates got at four p.m.: once it was an established fact that I was going to be going to Palestine, I would promise to send one or another of my classmates a kilo, or ten, or a hundred kilos, or a case, of oranges, that magical fruit we knew about from books; if he would give me half his snack, he would get, next year at the latest, a whole consignment of oranges, and as a *bona fides* of this deal in futures, I would let him have, right then, a little piece of my strip of film. Only one child was taken in: he gave me half his snack and instantly ran off to tell on me to the headmistress. I had stolen and I had lied. I was punished severely, but I no longer recall what the punishment consisted of.

This nebulous memory prompts hazy questions which I have never managed to clarify. How was it that during that period, lasting maybe the length of the summer holidays, and on that Christmas Eve, I was the only child in a school that in those days was virtually full up, not with sick children, for whom it was originally intended, but with child refugees? So where did the others go during holidays, and who gave them those afternoon snacks which I alone, inexplicably, did not get? And above all, how could I have known that I was supposed to be going to Palestine? It was a real plan that my grandmother and my aunt Esther put together, as they were probably convinced that my mother would never come back. My grandmother set much store by "the child" (as I learnt much later, that is how she and Esther referred to me) coming with her to Palestine, to live with her son Léon in Haifa. But Léon and his wife (who was also called Esther) already had three children, and they were so reluctant about adopting a fourth that Rose, my grandmother, ended up leaving on her own, long after the end of the war, in 1946.

In 1943–44 my grandmother had lodgings at Villard. A little later she went to live in a children's home at Lans and took me with her. I don't remember seeing her once during all my time at Collège Turenne (that doesn't mean she didn't come: it means I don't remember). The most logical explanation would be that I have shifted the whole scene by six months or a year, and that it happened at Lans. But the decor and the details of the memory, that attic, that playground where my disastrous deals were done, that catastrophe taking the shape of the headmistress bursting in, are, for me, specific to Collège Turenne and quite unrelated to the little boarding house at Lans, which is the site of another, equally strong, equally painful, if not more painful, memory of a fundamentally different kind.

TWENTY-SIX

The conception of children on W gives rise to a great celebration known as the Atlantiad.

W women are contained in Women's Quarters and guarded with great vigilance, not for fear of their escaping – they are meek in the extreme and have a somewhat fearful view of the outside world – but in order to protect them from the men: indeed, many Athletes, mostly among those banned from the Atlantiads by the merciless laws of W Sport, try almost every day, and in spite of the harsh penalties imposed for this kind of conduct, to break into the Women's Section and to get to the dormitories. The particular cast of mind prevailing in W society manifests itself, moreover, in the curious way this is dealt with: the severity of the punishment to which an Athlete is sentenced is in fact directly proportional to the distance between him and the women at the point of his arrest: if he is taken in proximity to the electric fence surrounding the Women's Quarters, he may well be executed on the spot; if he manages to cross the patrol zone behind it, he can get off with a few weeks in solitary; if he succeeds in negotiating the inner boundary wall, all he'll get is a caning: and if he should be so lucky as to reach the dormitories – no one ever has, but it is not theoretically impossible – he will be congratulated publicly in the Central Stadium and will be given the title of Honorary Casanova, which officially entitles him to take part in the next Atlantiad.

The number of women is quite restricted. It rarely goes beyond five hundred. It is the custom, in fact, to allow all male children to survive (unless they show some deformity at birth of the sort that would make them unable to compete, account being taken of the fact that in the pentathlon and the decathlon a minor physical defect is often considered more of an asset than a handicap) but only one girl child out of every five is kept.

Up to the age of thirteen or fourteen, girls and boys share the same life in the Youth Homes. Then boys are sent to the villages, where they become novices and subsequently Athletes, and the girls go on to the Women's Quarters. All day long they busy themselves with socially useful tasks: weaving costumes, tracksuits and standards, making shoes, sewing ceremonial garb, performing various cooking and housekeeping chores, unless, obviously, they are about to deliver or are busy with babes in arms for the first few months. They never leave Quarters, except for the Atlantiads.

Atlantiads are held about once a month. The women thought to be fertile are taken to the Central Stadium, their clothing is removed, and they are released onto the track, where they start to run as fast as they can. They are allowed a head start of half a lap before the best W Athletes, that is to say the best two in each event, making in all, as there are twenty-two events and four villages, one hundred and seventy-six men, are sent off in pursuit. One lap is usually all that the runners need to catch up with the women, and as a rule it is right in front of the podium, either on the cinder track or on the grass, that they get raped.

This special procedure, which makes the Atlantiads unlike any other W contest, has, as can be imagined, several noteworthy consequences. In the first place it completely deprives all the unseeded Athletes (even if they won in the preceding Spartakiad) and those who came third in the last ranking heats (for instance, Perkins in the W 400 metres, Shanzer in the North-W shot-put, Amstel in the North-West-W 100 metres, etc.) of any chance of getting a woman for as long as they remain third or, a fortiori, unseeded (and even if the third man has come first or second in a local championship, a selection trial or even an Olympic contest). In the second place, since the number of women is always less than 176 (in fact it is rarely over fifty), most Athletes entitled to run in the Atlantiad, often two-thirds of them, sometimes more, get absolutely nothing. Lastly, it is obvious that given the nature of the contest and the half-lap head start allowed to the women, the middle-distance or, marginally, the 400 metres sprinters are at a distinct advantage. 100 metres and 200 metres sprinters often run out of breath before reaching the goal, long-distance and marathon runners find it hard to dominate a race that is rarely longer than a lap, that is to say five hundred and fifty metres. As for the non-runners, the jumpers may sometimes stand a slim chance, but the putters, tossers and wrestlers are virtually ruled out from the start.

To make up for these differences and so as to establish a minimal degree of balance, Altantiad Administration has progressively relaxed the rules of the race and allowed practices which would obviously not be acceptable in any normal contest. That is how, first, tripping came to be permissible, then, more generally, all moves aimed at making a rival lose his balance: shouldering, elbowing, kneeing, single or double handpush, transcutaneous percussion of the popliteus in order to provoke an automatic reflex of the leg, etc. For some time there was an attempt to prohibit types of assault that were reckoned to be excessively violent, such as throttling, biting, uppercuts, rabbit punches – forearm smashes to the third spinal vertebra – head butts to the solar plexus (or "cannonballs"), ripping out of eyeballs, any sort of blow to the sexual organs, etc. But as such assaults became more and more common, it became harder and harder to stop them and in the end they were accepted as part of the rules. However, to prevent contestants hiding weapons in their clothes (not guns, which

Athletes are obviously forbidden to use, but for instance the leaded leather thongs used by the boxers, the javelin throwers' metal tips, the putters' shots, or whatever cutting tools, scissors, forks, or knives they might have been able to get hold of), which would make the contest degenerate too far and turn it into a slaughter with an unforeseeable outcome – after all, it is only the villages' and, in the last analysis, the Island's best sportsmen who are allowed into the Atlantiads – it was decreed that the combatants, like the women they pursue, should be entirely naked. The only allowance made – justified by the extent to which it is still a running race, even though it starts with a fair degree of bustle – is for shoes, whose spikes are honed down to particularly keen and cutting tips.

TWENTY-SEVEN

I do not remember exactly when or in what circumstances I left Collège Turenne. I think it was after the Germans had got to Villard and shortly before their major offensive against the Vercors.

All the same, one summer's day I was back on the road, with my grandmother. She was carrying a large suitcase, and I had a small one. It was hot. We stopped often; my grandmother sat on her case, and I sat on the ground or on a milestone. That went on for a markedly long time. I must have been eight and my grandmother at least sixty-five, and it took us an entire afternoon to cover the seven kilometres between Villard-de-Lans and Lans-en-Vercors.

The children's home we moved into was much smaller than Collège Turenne. I cannot remember its name or what it looked like and when I returned to Lans I tried but failed to identify it, as either I lacked any sense of familiarity anywhere or, on the other hand, I would decide that any old chalet was it and strain to winkle out of some architectural detail, out of the presence of a slide or an eave or a gate, the material of a memory.

It was not until much later that I learnt that my grandmother had been taken on at the home as a cook. As she hardly spoke French, and as her foreign accent could have made her dangerously noticeable, it was agreed she would pretend to be dumb.

I have only one memory of this boarding house. One day a little girl was found locked in the store cupboard where the brooms were kept. She had been there for several hours. Everybody claimed that I was the guilty one and insisted that I own up: even if I hadn't done it from malice, or even if I had done it without realizing it was bad, and all the more if I had done it not on purpose, but only inadvertently, locking the cupboard door without knowing I was locking the little girl in too, I had to confess: I had spent the whole afternoon in the playroom (I think it was not a very large room, with lino on the floor and three windows making a verandah), and consequently I was the only person who could have locked up the little girl. But I knew perfectly well that I hadn't done it, on purpose or not, and I refused to confess. I think I was sent to Coventry and no one spoke to me for several days.

Some time later – but this other event is not a separate memory, it remains inextricably tied to the foregoing – we were again in that same playroom. A bee settled on my left thigh. I got up with a start, and it stung me. My thigh swelled up massively (that was when I learnt what the difference is between wasps, which are fundamentally harmless creatures, and bees, whose stings can in certain cases be fatal; bumble bees don't sting; but hornets, which are fortunately uncommon, are to be feared even more than bees). For all my classmates, and especially for me, this sting was *proof* that I had locked up the little girl: the Good Lord had punished me.

TWENTY-EIGHT

No sports event on W, not even the ceremonial opening of the Olympiads, can offer a spectacle to compare with the Atlantiads.

Their unique attraction probably comes in large measure from the fact that unlike all the other contests, which are conducted with intense discipline and strictness, Atlantiads are placed under the sign of total liberty. They call for no Linesmen, no Timekeepers, no Referees. In ordinary races, be they heats or finals, the twelve competitors are brought to the starting line in mesh cages (somewhat similar to the stalls used for race horses) which are raised simultaneously when the Starter's pistol goes off (unless, for a joke, one of the Judges has decided to retard the release mechanism of one or two or even all the cages for a few seconds, thus provoking, on most occasions, quite spectacular incidents). In Atlantiads, the one hundred and seventy-six contestants are all bunched together in the starting area; electrified wire netting, several yards wide, stands on the track, separating them from the women. When the women have got far enough ahead, the Starter switches off the current and the men can set off in pursuit of their prey. But even in the strict sense of the word this is not the start of the race. The contest, that is to say the fight, actually begins well before then. A good third of the field has already been essentially eliminated, either because they have been knocked out and are lying unconscious on the ground or because the wounds they have suffered, especially foot and leg injuries caused by spiked shoes, have made them unable to run any distance, however short.

In the Atlantiads there is no one thing that might properly be called a strategy guaranteeing victory. Each participant has to try to assess his chances in terms of his individual strengths, and then has to decide on which line to take. A very good middle-distance runner who knows he can reach his top speed after three or four hundred metres obviously has an interest in being placed as far back from the starting line as possible: the fewer opponents there are behind him, the better his chances of not being assaulted before the off. On the other hand, boxers and shot-putters, who know they have virtually no chance in the race, try instead to eliminate as many opponents as they can, as fast as they can. Thus some try to protect themselves for as long as possible, others, on the contrary, attack straightaway. In between these two more or less well-defined groups, the main body of the field never really knows which technique would be best, even though for them the ideal would clearly be to offer up their most dangerous rivals – the best runners – to the often blind violence of the pugilists.

This simple framework is made considerably more complex by the possibility of pacts. The notion of a pact has no sense in the other contests: in them, Victory is unique and individual, and it would only be from fear of reprisals that a poorly placed competitor might give assistance, if he could, to the best-placed man from his village. But in Atlantiads, and this is one of their distinguishing features, there are as many winners as there are women to conquer, and since all the wins are identical to each other (it would obviously be utopian for any runner to covet any particular woman), it is perfectly possible for a group of contestants to club together against the others, up to the final share-out of the women. Such tactical alliances can take two forms, depending on whether the starters make pacts based on nationality (that is to say, village citizenship) or pacts based on their specialism. Though these two nuclei may conceivably coexist, they seldom do, but they often relay each *other, sometimes with terrifying speed, and it is always a stunning sight when a North-West-W hammer thrower (by definition Zacharie or Andereggen), for example, fights one of his colleagues from another village, such as Olafsson from North-W or Magnus from W, and then suddenly joins forces with him to fall on someone from his own village (Friedrich or von Kramer or Zannucci or Sanders, etc.).*

But these preliminary battles held in the starting area before the race proper are themselves only the final stage, the last act, the closing twists, of a war – it does not seem too strong a word here – which is no less furious and often murderous for having been waged off-track. The reason for this war is simple: the Atlantiad participants (the two front runners in each ranking heat) are known several days, and sometimes as much as three weeks, in advance, and from that point on every day, every hour, every minute presents an opportunity for a pending contestant to dispose of opponents and enhance his own chances of winning. Though this permanent strife, in which the competition proper is but a culminating point, is surely one of the great Laws of W life, it finds its richest field of application in the Atlantiads, inasmuch as the reward – a woman – is immediately associated with Winning.

Traps are laid, deals are set up, alliances are made and unmade in the Stadium passageways, in the changing rooms, in the showers, in the mess halls. The most experienced try to barter their good advice; a wrestler sells a favour: he'll pretend to knock you out, you'll be able to play dead until the Starter's pistol goes off. In bands of fifteen or twenty, unseeded Nignogs drawn by the mad hope of a usually paltry perk – half a cigarette, a few sugar lumps, a bar of chocolate, a bit of butter brought back from a banquet – attack a Champion from a proximate village and leave him for dead. Pitched battles break out at night in the dormitories. Athletes are drowned in sinks and lavatory pans.

The Administration is not unaware of this never-ending trade. Notices prohibiting it have been posted everywhere; they point out that Sports morality does not allow deals, that Victory cannot be bought. But no serious steps have ever been taken to put a stop to such practices. The Administration seems to be able to live with them. For the Officials, they are proof that Athletes are always on their marks, that not only on the track but everywhere and all the time the Law of W holds sway.

Other contests are held in total silence. The Race Manager is the person who raises his arm to signal the start of the cheering and chanting. At the Atlantiads, on the contrary, the crowd may or, rather, must yell its heart out, and the shouting, picked up by microphones, is amplified to maximum volume through loudspeakers placed all around the Stadium.

On the track as in the stands, and at the end of the race – when the survivors finally manage to lay their hands on their breathless prey – the shouting and yelling reaches such a paroxysm that you could almost take it for a riot.

TWENTY-NINE

The Liberation came; I have no visual memory of it or of any of its chapters or even of the waves of enthusiasm that accompanied and followed it and in which it is more than likely that I took part. I went back to Villard with my grandmother and lived with her for a few months in the tiny lodgings she had in the old part of the village.

At the start of the new school year I went to the village school, and it is that school year (maybe "Junior Form Two", in any case the equivalent of primary four) which today still marks the starting point of my own chronology: eight years old, class eight (like any other French child going through school in a normal manner), a kind of year zero preceded by the unknown (so when exactly did I learn to read, write and count?) but from which I can derive mechanically all that followed: 1945, Rue des Bauches, the Scholarship examination, to which my fear of fractions (how to find the common denominator) goes back; 1946, Lycée Claude-Bernard, first form, Latin; 1948, Greek; 1949, Collège Geoffroy-Saint-Hilaire, at Etampes, I have to repeat third form; I drop Greek and opt for German, etc).

I have virtually no recollection of the school itself except that it was the site of frantic trading in American badges (the best-known were yellow metal discs embossed with the letters US and a kind of medallion depicting two crossed rifles) and silk scarves made from parachute cloth. I know that one of my classmates was called Philippe Gardes (I have mentioned him before), and I have since learnt that Louis Argoud-Puix was probably also in the class.

It was perhaps that winter that for the first and last time in my life I had a run in a bobsleigh, along the main road that goes down the hill from Les Frimas to the centre of Villard. We didn't make it all the way; about halfway down, on a level with the Gardes' farmhouse, whilst the whole crew (there must have been seven or eight of us on the bob: it was dented and pretty rusty but of impressive size all the same) was leaning right, into the bend, I leaned to the left, and we ended up at the bottom of the gulley which runs beside that stretch of the road, after a fall of a few yards, fortunately softened by thick snow. I don't know whether this accident really happened to me or whether, as we have seen me do on other points, I invented or borrowed it, but in any event it stands as one of my favourite examples of my "frustrated left-handedness": I reckon, in fact, that I was born left-handed; at school I was forced to write with my right hand. This has resulted, in my case, not in a stammer (as apparently it often does) but in a slight lean of the head to the left (quite marked until only a few years ago) and above all in a more or less chronic and still undiminished inability to tell not just left from right (which was what stopped me passing my driving test: the examiner asked me to turn right, and I almost rammed a lorry on the left; it also helps to make me a fairly useless oarsman: I don't know which side to pull to turn the boat) but also the acute from the grave accent, concave from convex, the "larger than" sign (>) from the "smaller than" sign (<) and in general all terms that more or less approximately imply any kind of laterality and/or dichotomy (hyperbole/parabola, numerator/denominator, affective/ effective, dividend/divisor, caudal/rostral, metaphor/ metonymy, paradigm/syntagm, schizophrenia/paranoia, Capulet/Montagu, Whig/Tory, Guelph/Ghibelline, etc.); it also explains my fondness for mnemonics, whether for telling port from starboard by thinking of the word posh, or for remembering whether clocks are to be put forward or back ("Spring forward, Fall back"), or for distinguishing concave from convex by imagining a cave, or for remembering musical notation ("Every Good Boy Deserves Favour"), or for listing Roman emperors in order (Catcal, Clangalot, etc.) or merely for keeping French spelling rules straight: the hat of *cime* ("the top") falls to *abîme* ("the bottom").

Fairly soon after that, my grandmother and my aunt Esther went back to Paris. I went to stay with Esther's sister-in-law, my aunt Berthe; she had a fifteen-year-old son, Henri, and she lived in a villa below Villard, near the ice rink and the little ski run which was called, I think, Les Bains (there was another one called Les Clochettes and a third one, much harder and much further away, which was called La Côte 2000). I think it was a large house; it was a kind of chalet with a big wooden balcony. I had a lovely room with a full-size bed. Once I was ill and as a cure Berthe made me drink cherry-stalk tea, which tasted very nasty. Another time she cupped me, and for me cupping is still inextricably bound up with a cookery routine which Berthe performed regularly: employing a glass and a strict sequence designed to make the most economical use possible of the dough, she cut it into little discs which were then put on a greased baking tray to become, eventually, either shortbread or, after some even more tricky operations, small stuffed croissants.

THIRTY

A W child knows almost nothing of the world in which he will live. For the first fourteen years of his life, he is, so to speak, left to his own devices, no attempt being made to inculcate in him any of the traditional values of W society. He is not given a taste for Sport, he is not persuaded of the need for effort: he is not subjected to the harsh laws of competition. He is a child amongst children. No one nourishes in him the wish to overtake or overcome others; his spontaneous needs are met; no one rises against him and no one raises against him a wall of order, of logic, of the Law.

All W children are reared together; for the first months they stay with their mothers in the cosy warmth of the nurseries set up in the Women's Quarters. Then they are taken into the Youth Home. This is a long, single-storey building with huge windows letting in the daylight, located in a great park at some distance from the Fortress. The interior is a vast, unpartitioned room, that is a dormitory, playroom and refectory all in one; the kitchens are at one end, the showers and lavatories at the other. Boys and girls grow up together, mixing quite freely and happily. There can be as many as three thousand of them, five hundred girls and twenty-five hundred boys, but no more than a dozen educators in all are needed to supervise them. In fact, you can't properly call it supervision: the children aren't looked after at all, they aren't even really controlled. The adults exercise no pedagogic function, though occasionally they may find themselves giving advice or explanations. Their main task is hygienic, involving medical

137

*checks, the detection of diseases, preventative treatment and routine
surgery to deal with growths, tonsils, appendectomies, setting
of fractures, etc. The older children, the thirteen- and fourteen-
year-old adolescents, look after the youngest, teaching them how
to make beds, wash clothes, cook food, etc. All decide freely on
their timetables, their activities, and their games.*

*Of what goes on in the villages and stadiums they have only a
muddled knowledge based almost entirely on fantasy. The park
is huge and its boundaries are so overgrown that they don't even
know that insurmountable barriers — moats, electrified fences,
minefields — separate them from the adult world. They sometimes
hear far-off shouting, thunderclaps, trumpet blasts; they see thousands of coloured balloons floating by overhead, or magnificent
flocks of doves. They know these are the signs of great celebrations
which they will be allowed to join in one day. Sometimes they
act them out in great joyful round dances, or else, at night,
brandishing flaming torches, they rampage around in wild pro-
cessions until they fall on top of each other in a heap, breathless
and drunk with gaiety.*

*In the course of their fifteenth year, children leave the Home for
good; girls return to the Women's Quarters which they will only
ever leave for an Atlantiad, boys go on to the village which they
will come to serve as future Athletes.*

*A teenage boy often has a magical notion of the world he is about
to enter: the sadness he may feel on leaving his companions is
mitigated by the sure fact that he will soon see them again,
and it is with light-hearted impatience, sometimes even with
enthusiasm, that he climbs into the helicopter come to carry
him off.*

Once assigned to villages, children have at least three years as novices before they become Athletes. They join in the morning training sessions but not in the championships. The first six months of the noviciate, however, are spent in handcuffs and leg irons, and at night newcomers are chained to their bed, and often also gagged. This is what is called Quarantine and it is no exaggeration to say that it is the most painful period in the life of a W Sportsman, that all that follows – humiliation, insults, injustices, beatings – is, so to speak, almost as naught, has almost no weight, beside these first hours, these first weeks. Initial acquaintance with W life is, in truth, a somewhat frightening spectacle. Novices tour the Stadiums, the training camps, the cinder-tracks, the clubrooms; they are still unworried and confident youngsters whose lives have until now been bound up with the fraternal warmth of thousands of companions, and everything which they previously associated with visions of sumptuous feasts – the shouting, the triumphal music, the flights of white birds – now appears before them in an intolerable light. Then they see the cohort of the beaten returning, the exhausted, ashen-faced Athletes tottering under the weight of oaken yokes; they see them collapse onto the ground, where they lie with their mouths open, wheezing; they see them, a little later, tearing each other to pieces for a scrap of salami, a drop of water, a puff at a cigarette. They see, at dawn, the Winners returning, gorged with suet and rough liquor, slumping into their own vomit.

Thus ends the novice's first day. The following days will be spent in the same way. To begin with he does not grasp. Novices a little more senior than he sometimes try to explain, to tell him what goes on, how things work, what he must do and what he mustn't do. But usually they can't do it. How can you explain that what he is seeing is not anything horrific, not a nightmare, not something he will suddenly wake from, something he can rid his mind of? How can you explain that this is life, real life, this is what there'll be every day, this is what there is, and nothing else, that it's pointless believing something else exists or to pretend to believe in something else, that it's not even worth your time trying to hide it, or to cloak it, it's not even worth your time pretending to believe there must be something behind it, or beneath it, or above it? That's what there is, and that's all. There are competitions every day, where you Win or Lose. You have to fight to live. There is no alternative. It is not possible to close your eyes to it, it is not possible to say no. There's no recourse, no mercy, no salvation to be had from anyone. There's not even any hope that time will sort things out. There's this, there's what you've seen, and now and again it will be less horrible than what you've seen and now and again it will be much more horrible than what you've seen. But wherever you turn your eyes, that's what you will see, you will not see anything else, and that is the only thing that will turn out to be true.

But even the most senior Athletes, even the doddery veterans who clown on the track in between races and are fed rotten vegetable stalks by the hilarious crowd, even they still believe that there is something else, that the sky can be bluer, the soup better, the Law less harsh; they believe that merit will be rewarded, that victory will smile on them, and be wonderful.

Faster, higher, stronger. Gradually, over the months of Quarantine, the proud Olympic motto is imprinted in the novices' minds. Very few attempt suicide, very few go really mad. Some never stop howling, but most of them keep silent, obstinately.

THIRTY-ONE

My first memories of reading date from this period. Lying flat on my stomach on my bed, I devoured the books my cousin Henri gave me to read.

One of these books was a serial novel. I think it was called *A Paris Lad Goes Round the World* (a work by that title does exist, but there are many very similar ones: *A Paris Lad Goes Round France, A Boy of Fifteen Goes Round the World, Two Children Go Round France*, etc.). It wasn't one of those fat red books like the Hetzel edition of Jules Verne, but rather a thick paper-bound tome made up of many instalments, each with its own illustrated coverpage. One of these covers depicted a child of about fifteen walking along a very narrow path cut halfway up in the side of a high cliff plunging down into an unfathomable gulley. This classic image of adventure stories (and of Westerns) has remained so familiar to me that I still think I saw more or less identical ones in books I read much later – such as *The Carpathian Castle* or *Mathias Sandorf* – in which, not long ago, I hunted for them without success.

The second book was *Michael, the Circus Dog*, at least one of whose episodes imprinted itself in my memory: an athlete is about to be drawn asunder by four horses, but in actual fact the horses are pulling not on the athlete's limbs but on four steel cables crossed over in an X and camouflaged by the athlete's costume; he smiles under this fake torture, but the circus director demands that he make a show of the most excruciating pain.

The third book, *Twenty Years After*, made an impression on me which my memory has enlarged out of all proportion, perhaps because it is the only one of these three books which I have re-read since, and re-read occasionally even today. It feels as though I knew this book by heart and that I took in so many details that re-reading it was simply a matter of checking that they were still in their proper places: the silver-gilt corners on Mazarin's table, Porthos's letter tucked away for fifteen years in a pocket in one of d'Artagnan's old doublets; Aramis's quadrangle in his convent; Grimaud's toolroll, thanks to which it is learnt that the barrels are full not of beer but of gunpowder; the incense paper d'Artagnan burns in his horse's ear; the way Porthos, who has still got a hefty fist (the size of a mutton chop, if I'm not mistaken), turns some fire-tongs into a corkscrew; the picture book which the young Louis XIV is looking at when d'Artagnan comes to fetch him away from Paris; Planchet in hiding with d'Artagnan's landlady and speaking Flemish to pretend he is her brother; the peasant carting wood and telling d'Artagnan the way to Château de La Fère in impeccable French; the unyielding hatred of Mordaunt when he asks Cromwell for the right to replace the hangman kidnapped by the Musketeers; and a hundred other episodes, whole chunks of story or mere turns of phrase which feel not only as if I had always known them but, much more, as if they were, to my mind, virtually part of history: an inexhaustible fount of memory, of material for rumination and of a kind of certainty: the words were where they should be, and the books told a story you could follow; you could re-read, and, on re-reading, re-encounter, enhanced by the certainty that you would encounter those words again, the impression you had felt the first time. This pleasure has never ceased for me; I do not read much, but I have never stopped re-reading Flaubert and Jules Verne, Roussel and Kafka, Leiris and Queneau; I re-read the books I love and I love the books I re-read, and each time it is the same enjoyment, whether I re-read twenty pages, three chapters, or the whole book: an enjoyment of complicity, of collusion, or more especially, and in addition, of having in the end found kin again.

There was however something striking about those first three books: they were all in effect incomplete, they presupposed other absent and unfindable books. The adventures of the *Paris Lad* were unfinished (there must have been a missing second volume); Michael, the *Circus Dog*, had a brother by the name of Jerry, who was the hero of island adventures I knew nothing about; and my cousin Henri possessed neither *The Three Musketeers* nor *The Vicomte de Bragelonne or, Ten Years Later*, which thus appeared to me to be bibliographic rarities, priceless books which I could only hope one day to be able to borrow. (This belief was quickly laid to rest as far as *The Three Musketeers* was concerned, but it lived on for several years with respect to *The Vicomte de Bragelonne*: I remember that in order to read it I borrowed it from a municipal library and I was almost surprised when I saw it in bookshops in early paperback editions, first in the Marabout series and later in Livre de Poche).

Henri had read *The Three Musketeers* and *The Vicomte de Bragelonne* and also, I believe, *The Lady of Montsoreau*; he

143

didn't remember *The Three Musketeers* terribly well (but well enough, I think, to explain what was essential for a proper understanding of *Twenty Years After*, for instance who Rochefort was, or Bonacieux – "that scoundrel Bonacieux" – or the Lady de Winter whom Mordaunt strives with such fury to avenge, but he was still very much under the spell of *The Vicomte de Bragelonne*: thus I learnt the mortal ends of characters (except for Aramis, who becomes a bishop) whose first and last adventures I knew nothing about: Porthos crushed by a boulder he can no longer support, Athos in his bed at the very instant that his son Raoul falls in Algeria, d'Artagnan swept off by a cannonball at the siege of Maestricht, just after being appointed *maréchal*.

I was transported most, and in the literal sense as well, by the death of d'Artagnan, since Henri told it and, with my assistance, acted out its main episodes whilst pushing me around in a little handcart on our long tramps around and about Villard from one farmyard to another to obtain supplies of eggs, milk and butter (I remember the wooden moulds that were used for making the blocks of butter, and the sharpness of the stamping marks – a little cow, a flower or a rosette – that they left on butter still robed in whitish droplets).

★

By dint of nagging, in the end I got Henri to teach me the game of battleships and cruisers. One day when he felt like giving me a special treat, he threw himself into the manufacture of two large draughts boards and the requisite ship tokens, which should have allowed us to engage in serious combat. He had nearly got to the end of this finicky labour, over which he expended so much care that I took it for fervour, probably because it corresponded to the fervour of my own expectation, when, one morning when I suppose I was being particularly exasperating, he flew into a rage as inexplicable as it was violent, and smashed and trampled those precious boards to pieces. On several occasions, over the following years, I reminded Henri of this incident, pointing out to him each time how completely impossible, illogical and almost unreal it had seemed to me, recalling each time for myself the impression of disbelief I had felt on seeing those boards turned to shreds. Each time, Henri expressed surprise that this outburst of adolescent anger had made such an impression on me: it seems to me, however, that what I deduced from this unbelievable act was not that Henri was just a child, but rather, more darkly, that he was not, was no longer, the infallible being, the model, the repository of knowledge and the dispenser of certainty which he of all people simply had to remain for me.

THIRTY-TWO

After six months' Quarantine, the newcomer is officially declared a novice. This promotion is marked by two events. The first is an induction ceremony which takes place in the Central Stadium in the presence of the whole body of Athletes: the handcuffs, leg irons and balls are taken off the youngsters, and each is handed the insignia of his new role: a large triangle of white cloth which he sews, with the apex at the top, on the back of his tracksuit. A Sub-Race Manager or a Timekeeper makes a little speech in words which hardly ever vary from one ceremony to another or from one Official to another: the future Athletes are welcomed, the virtues of Sport are lauded, and the main principles of the Olympic Ideal are gone over. Then, to close the ceremony, Athletes and novices join together in a friendly contest, that is to say, a contest whose results are not recorded and give rise to no rewards.

The second event is far more private and takes place in the village clubrooms. Originally a secret and clandestine ritual, it was eventually recognized by the Administration, which, as is its wont, did not try to prohibit it but was satisfied instead with codifying its operation. The aim of the ritual is to select an Athlete to be the novice's protector, that is to say the person responsible for his training, for showing him around the Stadiums, for teaching him the techniques of Sport, the social rules, the external marks of respect, the customs of his village, etc. Obviously he is the one who comes to the novice's aid every time he is threatened. In

146

return, a novice serves his appointed guardian with devotion and gratitude: he makes his bed every morning, brings him his bowl of porridge, washes his linen and his mess-tin and serves him his mid-day meal; he keeps the sportsman's gear, his trunks and his running shoes in good order. Additionally, he serves as his catamite.

Only the seeded, of course, can have the honour of protecting a novice. One may recall that in each village there are 330 Athletes of whom 66 are seeded in regular fashion, that is to say, who have gained their names in ranking heats, and maybe at most a score of Nignogs who have managed to grab an identity by winning in a Spartakiad. Now the total number of novices fluctuates, as we have seen, between 50 and 70. Thus there could be roughly as many Champion-protectors as novice-protégés. But to think that things could be so arranged would reveal a profound misapprehension of the nature of W society. In fact, the selection of guardians is determined by the outcome of single combat between the village's two top Champions, which is to say, two men who are at least Olympic Champions, with names prefixed by the definite article (the Kekkonen, the Jones, the MacMillan, etc). If there are several Olympic Champions in a village (which there often are, since there are 22 Olympic Champions and 4 villages) priority is given to the winners of the so-called noble disciplines: first the contests of running speed, 100 metres, 200 metres, 400 metres, then the high jump, the long jump, 110 metres hurdles, then the middle-distance events, etc., down to, as a last resort, the pentathlon and decathlon men.

As a general rule, therefore, most novices have as their appointed guardian one or another of these two super-Champions. It can happen that the novices are fought over bitterly and that a bloody battle takes place over their acquisition, but most often they are shared out by unspoken agreement: the Champions take turns, *according to supply, selecting from the stock of novices, and their single combat is kept down to a few pointed harangues and a sham clinch.*

Thus it can easily be seen how this institution, which originally dealt only with the relations between seniors and freshmen, modelled somewhat on what normally happens in high schools and army regiments, came on W to be the base of a complex vertical structure, of a hierarchical system involving all the Sportsmen in a village in a set of interlocking relationships, and whose operations constitute the entirety of the villages' social life. The reigning protectors have no real use for their surfeit of underlings; they keep two or three for themselves and farm out the services of the rest to other Athletes. The end result is therefore the establishment of a veritable system of patronage, which the two top Champions manipulate to suit themselves.

At the purely local level, the protecting Champions' power is immense and their chances of survival are far higher than other Athletes'. Through systematic drubbings, by harassing them at the hands of their novices and their Nignogs, by stopping them eating, by stopping them sleeping, they can wear out those of their co-villagers from whom they have the most to fear, those seeded immediately after them in their event, who breathe down their necks in each contest, and for whom, they know, Victory would signal the start of a merciless revenge.

The patronage system, though, is as fragile as it is fierce. An opponent's determination or a Referee's whim can in one split second rob a Champion of the names he fought so hard to win and defended so ferociously. And the throng of his followers will turn against him to go and beg morsels, sugar lumps and smiles from the new Victors.

148

THIRTY-THREE

At aunt Berthe's there was also a big Larousse dictionary in two volumes. Perhaps that is where I first learned to love dictionaries. I can hardly remember that one any more except for a colour plate entitled "Flags", which reproduced the ensigns of most, if not all of the sovereign states in the world, including San Marino and the Vatican. I probably looked at this plate with particular attention only because throughout this period Henri and I made a whole set of flags in the colours of America, Britain, France and Russia, on the one hand, and Germany on the other (I don't remember there being any others, for Canada or Yugoslavia, for instance) which we used to mark up, on a big map of Europe pinned to the wall, the triumphant advance of the Allied armies as reported to us by our daily newspaper, *Les Allobroges* (I was proud of knowing that *Allobroges* was the name of the peoples who inhabited Savoy and Dauphiné in pre-Roman times). The flags stood for armies or even for army corps or divisions, the main idea being, apparently, that each flag should have on it a general's name. I have forgotten almost all those generals' names now, even if I do still know who Zhukov, Eisenhower, Montgomery, Patton and Omar Bradley were. My favourite was General de Larminat. I also had a soft spot for Thierry d'Argenlieu, not just because he was the only admiral I had heard of but also because there was a rumour that he was a monk.

★

Another one of my memories concerns François Billoux, who was also a sort of idol for me, especially once I managed to stop confusing him with François Billon. There was an enormous public meeting in Villard to mark his passing through. The square, which had a fountain in the middle, now gone, was packed with people. Henri and I were able to get near the rostrum. Henri had in his hand Ilya Ehrenburg's book *The Fall of Paris* (there was something about that book which amazed me, which I could not grasp: it was a book written by a Russian but set in Paris; in French translation it wasn't noticeable, but in the original Russian, how did you write it, and what effect did it have on the reader, when you had, for instance, "Rue Cujas", or "Rue Soufflot"?). Henri held out the book to François Billoux, who gave it back with his autograph. I, for my part, probably having more luck than I'd had with the bishop, succeeded in getting my hand shaken.

★

I often went to the square to fetch the newspaper (the newsagent-cum-tobacconist-cum-souvenirs-and-postcards shop is still in the same place). One day in May 1945 I found the square again packed with people, and I had great difficulty in getting into the shop to buy the paper. I ran home through streets thronging with excited crowds, waving *Les Allobroges* in my outstretched hand and yelling for all I was worth, "Japan has capitulated!"

★

One evening we went to the cinema. There was Henri, Berthe, Robert, Henri's father who had just come down from Paris, I think, to help us go back up, and me. The film was called *The Great White Silence*, and Henri was in

150

raptures about going to see it, since he remembered a marvellous story by Curwood that had the same title, and all day long he told me about pack ice and Eskimos, huskies and snowshoes, Klondike and Labrador. But the very first frames brought us a ghastly disappointment: the great white desert was not the Far North but the Sahara, where a young officer by the name of Charles de Foucauld, weary of the wild times he'd had with disreputable women (he drank champagne out of their shoes), was becoming a missionary: this was despite the entreaties of his friend General Laperrine, who was still only a captain and who reached him with his Arab unit too late to save him from the wicked Tuareg (singular: Tarki) besieging his blockhouse. I remember the death of Charles de Foucauld: he is tied to a post, the fatal bullet has gone straight through his eye, and blood runs down his cheek.

THIRTY-FOUR

*The boundary separating Sportsmen from Officials is all the
more marked for not being absolutely insurmountable. W Laws,
normally so laconic, and whose very silence is a mortal threat to
the Athletes under its yoke, are astonishingly wordy on this point:
they give meticulous, indulgent, almost unstinting descriptions of
every circumstance under which an Athlete, after his years of
competitive sport, can accede to a position of responsibility either
in his Village, as a Team Manager, Trainer, masseur, showerer,
hairdresser, etc., or in the Stadiums, where a host of minor jobs,
which follow a strict pecking order, may be offered him: server,
shouter, sweeper, dovekeeper, torch or standbearer, mascot,
musician, calligrapher, stand inspector, etc.*

*At first sight it does not appear to be very difficult for an Athlete
to meet the conditions for appointment to any of these positions
and thus to enjoy the perks associated with them, which, however
minute they may seem (exemption from chores, shower entitlement, personalized billet, free access to the Stadiums, to changing
rooms, banqueting halls, etc.), often turn out to be essential just
for the Veteran's survival. There is first of all a whole system
of points, bonuses and gratuities that are accumulated over an
Athlete's entire career: they are totted up so that in theory, if
an Athlete has given four years' steady showing, then as an
ex-Champion he is more or less assured of automatic promotion
to a privileged post. Then there are various combinations of wins
which allow the Winners to cross the line, to jump the barrier,*

even sooner: in three years if the Athlete gets a Pair Royal, that is to say if he comes second or third three times in a row in the Olympiads; in two years if he wins a Double Crown: two Olympic wins in succession, an achievement reckoned as the most glorious of all, but no instance of which has ever been recorded in the history of W; or even in one year, in a single season, if he gets a Full House (first place in the ranking heats, in both Local Championships, and in the Selection Trial) or a Hat Trick (first in the ranking heats, first in the Selection, first in the Olympiad), a combination that would seem statistically more probable, but which actually occurs extremely seldom. Finally, there are, in tune with the spirit of W life itself, various systems apparently based on pure chance: a miserable Athlete, a chronic Nignog, incapable of anything like a decent performance, incapable of earning a Name, can become an Official overnight: all it takes is, for example, for the number of his vest to match the Winner's time.

The multiplicity of these Laws, their detail, and the great number and variety of the opportunities thus created, could lead one to believe that it really takes very little for an Athlete to become an Official, as if the Laws of W, by asserting the wish to reward high sporting achievement as well as steady service and just good luck, wanted to give the impression that Athletes and Officials belonged to the same Race, to the same world; as if they were all one family united by a single goal, the greater glory of Sport alone; as if there were nothing that really separated them: the contestants compete and redouble their efforts on the cinders; thronging the stands, on their feet, the crowd of their comrades cheers them on or boos them down; the Officials sit in the Stalls, and the same spirit moves them, the same combat thrills them, the same flame burns in them!

But we know the world of W well enough to grasp that its most lenient Laws are but the expression of a greater and more savage irony. The apparent leniency of the rules governing promotion to official positions always comes up against the whimsicality of the Hierarchy: what a Timekeeper proposes, a Referee may refuse; what a Referee promises, a Judge may forbid; what a Judge proposes, a Manager disposes; what one Manager grants, another may disallow. High Officials have all the power; they can sanction, just as they can veto; they can uphold the choice of fate, or choose a different fatality, at random; they make the decisions, and they can change them at any time.

It is never certain that at the end of his career an Athlete will manage to become an Official and it is even more uncertain that he will remain one. But in any case, there is no other way out. Veterans who are expelled from their teams and do not get posts, the ones who are called packmules, have no rights and no protection at all. Dormitories, refectories, showers and changing rooms are out of bounds. They are not entitled to speak, they are not entitled to sit down. They are often stripped of their tracksuits and shoes. They gather in clusters near the dustbins, they loiter at night by the gallows, trying, in spite of the Guards who shoot them down on sight, to tear morsels of flesh from the rotting corpses of the losers who have been stoned and hanged. They huddle together in tight bunches, forlornly attempting to keep warm and to snatch from the icy night a moment of sleep.

The petty officials, to tell the truth, do not have much to do: the shower operators turn their taps to boiling or freezing without paying too much attention; the hairdressers take a bit off with their clippers; the stand inspectors crack their long whips; the shouters give the signal for the applause and the booing to start.

But the Men must stand up and fall in. They must get out of the compounds – Raus! Raus! – they must start running – Schnell! Schnell! – they must come into the Stadium in impeccable order!

Petty officials, whatever their rank, are all-powerful before Athletes. And they impose respect for the harsh Laws of Sport with a savagery that is magnified ten times over by terror. For though they are better fed and better clothed, though they sleep better and are more relaxed, their fate nonetheless forever hangs on a Manager's cross glance, on a shadow crossing a Referee's brow, on a Judge's mood or prank.

THIRTY-FIVE

Before going to Paris we all stopped for a whole day in Grenoble. We didn't go on the cable car up to the Grande Chartreuse; it wasn't working anyway. Instead, Henri and I went to a tiny cinema called, I think, Le Studio; it was a lovely auditorium, with a carpet and wide armchair seats, really very different from the barns, community halls and suchlike that up until then had been my cinema houses. We saw *The Private Life of Henry VIII*, directed by Alexander Korda, starring Charles Laughton. That is, I think, where I first saw and heard the majestic striking of the gong preceding the credits in films made by Rank. Of the film itself only one scene has stuck: the one where the aged king, a little doddery but just as magnificently dressed and still just as gluttonous as ever, out of sight of his umpteenth wife (who makes him tremble like a little boy) voraciously guzzles a whole chicken all by himself.

The journey up to Paris took a very long time. Henri taught me to count the kilometres by observing to the outside edge of the right-hand track (when travelling towards Paris; they are virtually impossible to observe when travelling from Paris since the signs are then too close to the carriage you're looking out from) the signboards with white figures on blue which mark the number of kilometres to go to Paris, one-hundred-metre divisions being marked by white stakes, except the fifth, which is red. It is a habit I've kept, and I don't believe I've made a train journey since then, of sixty minutes or six hours, without amusing myself by watching the hundred metres, the half-kilometres and the kilometres march past at speeds considerably greater now than on that return journey.

We set off one evening. We got to Paris in the afternoon of the following day. My aunt Esther and my uncle David were waiting for us on the platform. As we came out of the station I asked what that monument was called: I was told that it wasn't a monument, just the Gare de Lyon.

We got into my uncle's black 11HP Citroen. We took Henri and his parents to their home in Avenue Junot (the Duke d'Abrantès) in Montmartre, then we went home to Rue de l'Assomption.

Two days later my aunt sent me to the end of the street to get the bread. As I came out of the baker's shop I turned the wrong way, and instead of going back up Rue de l'Assomption I went down Rue de Boulainvilliers: it took me more than an hour to find my way back home.

Later on, I went to primary school in Rue des Bauches. Later on, I went to a Christmas treat given by Canadian soldiers; I don't recall which toy I got from the share-out, except that it wasn't one of the ones I had set my heart on. Later on, carrying a great red sheaf of flowers, marching beside two other children carrying, respectively, a blue and a white sheaf of flowers, I paraded in front of a general.

Later on, my aunt took me to see an exhibition about concentration camps. It was being held somewhere near La Motte-Picquet-Grenelle (that same day, I learnt there were metro stations that were not underground but on stilts). I remember the photographs of the walls of the gas chambers showing scratchmarks made by the victims' fingernails, and a set of chessmen made from bits of bread.

THIRTY-SIX

A W Athlete has scarcely any control over his life. He has nothing to expect from the passing of time. Neither the alternation of days and nights nor the seasons' round will come to his aid. The fog of winter nights, the icy rain of spring, the torrid heat of summer afternoons afflict him equally. Of course he may expect Victory to improve his lot: but Victory is so rare and so often a mockery! The life of an Athlete of W is but a single, endless, furious striving, a pointless, debilitating pursuit of that unreal instant when triumph can bring rest. How many hundreds, how many thousands of hours of crushing effort for one second's serenity, one second of calm? How many weeks, how many months of exhaustion for one hour's relaxation?

Run. Run on cinders, run through the marshes, run in the mud. Run, jump, put the shot. Crawl. Bend your knees, up again. Up again, bend your knees. Do it very fast now, get the speed up. Run in a circle, lie down flat, crawl, get up, start running. Stand still, to attention, for hours, for days, for days and nights. Flat on your stomach! On your feet! Get dressed! Get undressed! Get dressed! Get undressed! Run! Jump! Crawl! On your knees!

Submerged in a world unchecked, with no knowledge of the Laws that crush him, a torturer or a victim of his co-villagers, under the scornful and sarcastic eyes of the Judges, the W Athlete does not know where his real enemies are, does not know that he could beat them or that such a win would be the only true Victory he could score, the only one which would liberate him. But his own life and death seem to him ineluctable, inscribed once and for all in an unspeakable fate.

There are two worlds, the world of the Masters and the world of slaves. The Masters are unreachable, and the slaves tear at each other. But an Athlete of W does not even know that. He would rather believe in his Star. He waits for luck to smile on him. One day the Gods will be for him, he'll draw the lucky number, he'll be the one whom chance will choose to carry the Olympic Flame to the Central Pyre, which, as it will give him the rank of Official Flamesman, will exempt him forever from all chores and, in theory, provide him with permanent protection. And it does indeed seem as though all his energy were devoted to simply waiting for that alone, to that single hope of a paltry miracle which will get him out of beatings, whippings, humiliation, fear. One of the ultimate features of W society is that fate is constantly being questioned: with bits of bread laboriously rolled between their fingers, Sportsmen make themselves dibs or little dice. They read the meaning of the flights of birds, of the shapes of clouds and puddles, of falling leaves. They collect talismans: a spike from an Olympic Champion's running shoe, a hanged man's fingernail. Sets of playing cards and tarot cards go the rounds of the barracks: games of chance settle the share-outs of bedding, of rations and of chores. A whole system of clandestine gambling, deviously controlled by the Administration through its petty officials, is attached to the Competitions. Anyone who guesses the registration numbers of the first three in an Olympic Event in their correct order is entitled to all the winners' privileges; anyone who gets the right numbers but in a different order is invited to join in their triumphal banquet.

Bands in bespangled uniforms play Beethoven's Ninth. Thousands of doves and coloured balloons are launched into the air. Behind huge, wind-whipped standards displaying the entwined circles, the Gods of the Stadium process on to the track in impeccable columns, their arms stretched out towards the official stalls where the great Dignitaries of W acknowledge them.

If you just look at the Athletes, if you just look: in their striped gear they look like caricatures of turn-of-the-century sportsmen as, with their elbows in, they lunge into a grotesque sprint; if you just look at the shot-putters, who have cannonballs for shot, at the jumpers with their ankles tied, at the long jumpers thudding into a sandpit filled with manure; if you just look at the wrestlers, tarred and feathered, if you just look at the long-distance runners running three-legged or on all fours, if you just look at the clapped-out, shivering survivors of the marathon, hobbling between two serried ranks of Line Judges armed with sticks and cudgels, if you just look and see these Athletes of skin and bone, ashen-faced, their backs permanently bent, their skulls bald and shiny, their eyes full of panic, and their sores suppurating, if you see all these indelible marks of humiliation without end, of boundless terror, all of it evidence, administered every hour, every day, every instant, of conscious, organized, structured oppression; if you just look and see the workings of this huge machine, each cog of which contributes with implacable efficiency to the systematic annihilation of men, then it should come as no great surprise that the performances put up are utterly mediocre: the 100 metres is run in 23.4", the 200 metres in 51"; the best high jumper has never exceeded 1.30 metres.

★

When someone gets in one day to the Fortress he will find first of all nothing but a sequence of dim, long, empty rooms. The sound of his footsteps echoing under the tall concrete roof supports will fill him with fear, but he must keep on going for a long time until he discovers, deep down in the depths of the earth, the subterranean remnants of a world he will think he had forgotten: piles of gold teeth, rings and spectacles, thousands and thousands of clothes in heaps, dusty card indexes, and stocks of poor-quality soap . . .

THIRTY-SEVEN

For years I did drawings of sportsmen with stiff bodies and inhuman facial features: I described their unending combats meticulously: I listed persistently their endless titles.

Years and years later, in David Rousset's *Univers concentra-tionnaire*, I read the following:

> The structure of punishment camps is determined by two fundamental policies: no work but "sport", and derisory feeding. The majority of inmates do no work at all, which means that work, even the hardest work, is seen as skiving off. Even the least job has to be done at top speed. Beatings, regular fare in "normal" camps, are here everyday trifles controlling every hour of the day and sometimes of the night as well. One of the games consists of making the prisoners dress and undress several times a day, very fast and beneath the cosh; or again, making them run in and out of the Block whilst two SS stand at the door and hit the Haeftlinge on the head with their Gummi truncheons. In the small rectangular concrete yard, anything can be turned to sport: making men turn round very fast, under the whip, for hours on end; organizing a bunny-hop race, with the slowest to be thrown in the pond beneath the Homeric guffaws of the SS: having them repeat endlessly the exercise that consists of squatting on your heels, and

then standing again, very fast, with both arms held out horizontally; forcing them to do press-ups fast (always fast, fast, *Schnell, los Mensch*), in the mud, up and down again a hundred times in a row, and then making them run to drench themselves in water to get clean, and keeping them in wet clothes for twenty-four hours.

★

I have forgotten what reasons I had at the age of twelve for choosing Tierra del Fuego as the site of W. Pinochet's Fascists have provided my fantasy with a final echo: several of the islands in that area are today deportation camps.

PARIS–CARROS–BLÉVY

1970 – 1974

W

was set in Linotron Bembo, a typeface based on the types used by Venetian scholar-publisher Aldus Manutius in the printing of *De Aetna*, written by Pietro Bembo and published in 1495. The original characters were cut in 1490 by Francesco Griffo who, at Aldus's request, later cut the first italic types. Originally adapted by the English Monotype Company, Bembo is one of the most elegant, readable, and widely used of all book faces.

Typeset by Rowland Phototypesetting, Bury St. Edmunds, Suffolk, England. Printed and bound by Maple-Vail Book Manufacturing Group, Binghamton, New York.